Night Shift in Barcelona

Welcome to Santa Aelina University Hospital…

As night falls on Barcelona's busiest hospital, its bustling wards transform… From the hush-filled NICU to the tense operating theater, the Spanish city might be fast asleep, but St. Aelina's night shift team are *always* on standby for their patients—and each other! And in the heat of the Mediterranean night, that mix of drama and dedication might hand the hardworking staff a chance at summer love!

Set your alarm and join the night shift with…

The Night They Never Forgot by Scarlet Wilson

Their Barcelona Baby Bombshell by Traci Douglass

Their Marriage Worth Fighting For by Louisa Heaton

From Wedding Guest to Bride? by Tina Beckett

Dear Reader,

When I was asked to take part in this continuity, I was thrilled. What story would I be assigned? Who were my hero and heroine? When I discovered that I had been given Grace and Diego Rivas, a married couple torn apart by heartbreaking loss, I was glad to be able to write their story.

Early miscarriage is something that some couples feel they're not allowed to grieve for. That it wasn't a baby yet. But for anyone who has experienced miscarriage, early or otherwise, then they know just how devastating it can be. Losing a longed-for pregnancy stops time. It stops hearts. It shakes the ground beneath the feet of even the strongest love.

Grace and Diego are a couple who have gone through this, and I couldn't wait to write their story to give them the happy ending they deserved.

It made me wish I could write a happy ending for everyone.

I hope you enjoy their marriage-reunited story.

Warmest wishes,

Louisa xxx

THEIR MARRIAGE WORTH FIGHTING FOR

LOUISA HEATON

MEDICAL
ROMANCE

Special thanks and acknowledgment are given to Louisa Heaton
for her contribution to the Night Shift in Barcelona miniseries.

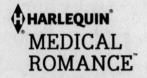

HARLEQUIN®
MEDICAL
ROMANCE™

Recycling programs
for this product may
not exist in your area.

ISBN-13: 978-1-335-73726-7

Their Marriage Worth Fighting For

Louisa Heaton lives on Hayling Island, Hampshire, with her husband, four children and a small zoo. She has worked in various roles in the health industry—most recently four years as a community first responder, answering 999 calls. When not writing, Louisa enjoys other creative pursuits, including reading, quilting and patchwork—usually instead of the things she *ought* to be doing!

Books by Louisa Heaton

Harlequin Medical Romance

Reunited at St. Barnabas's Hospital

Twins for the Neurosurgeon

A Child to Heal Them
Saving the Single Dad Doc
Their Unexpected Babies
The Prince's Cinderella Doc
Pregnant by the Single Dad Doc
Healed by His Secret Baby
The Icelandic Doc's Baby Surprise
Risking Her Heart on the Trauma Doc
A Baby to Rescue Their Hearts
A GP Worth Staying For
Their Marriage Meant To Be

Visit the Author Profile page at Harlequin.com.

For a baby I never got to meet xxx

CHAPTER ONE

THE ORANGE-PINK GLOW of the setting sun glided across the façade of the beautiful St Aelina's Hospital as Grace Rivas let out a deep, pent-up breath. A breath that was meant to steady her. To help her try to contain her nerves. A breath that was supposed to make her gird her loins, to prepare her for what waited inside.

Who waited inside.

She'd not called Diego to say she was back. It didn't feel right with the way things had been left. What were they? Husband and wife legally, yes, but *friends*? People who called one another up just to say hi? People who would rush into each other's arms, the way they'd used to? No. They were nothing that even came *close* to that.

That last argument before she'd left to visit her Aunt Felicity in Cornwall had been Heart-rending. The kind of argument that signalled the end of a relationship. And when you ended a relationship and then went away you didn't call that person when you got back home, because technically they weren't in your life any more.

She was not proud of the way she'd behaved. The lengths she had gone to in her desperation. The way she'd shouted. Ranted. Raved. Desperate for him to *say* something. To *do* something. To *react* to anything. Hoping beyond hope that somehow her words would get through that thick, impenetrable skull of his and he would call her *mi amor*, pull her close, kiss the top of her head and whisper into her hair that they would be okay. That he understood. That they would get through this. That they could deal with all the crap that life had thrown at them and come out on the other side somehow better, stronger than they'd been before.

Only he hadn't done any of that. He'd just stood there. Listening. Looking sad. Looking like a berated child. Looking sorry, but not actually saying it, his lips pressed together so tightly, so grimly, it had almost been as if he was biting them. Stopping himself from speaking. He'd just stood there and taken the full force, the full brunt of her fury and her rage.

Oh, how she wished he'd said something! *Anything!* To show her that there was still some chance they could pull themselves through that quagmire of anger.

But his silence, his inability to salvage anything from their relationship, had caused her to throw her hands up in frustration and storm past him, slamming the bedroom door behind her so that she could check her luggage one last time, knowing she couldn't miss her flight back to England. Especially because she'd be going *alone* now.

She hadn't heard him leave. Maybe because she'd been too busy muffling her sobs. But when she'd finally emerged, pulling her luggage behind her, expecting one last tearful goodbye, maybe even a last attempt to turn things around and save their relationship, she'd found a note on the kitchen counter.

I think it's best if I move into staff accommodation at the hospital.
For now.
D

Just *D*.

No kisses.

No, *let's talk when you get back*. Nothing. Grace had scrunched the note up in anger and tossed it into the bin.

Now, even thinking about that night caused a sour sensation in her stomach, and she had to swallow hard and look up at St Aelina's and try to remember the joy of this place.

The way it was lit up at night was particularly beautiful. Like another world. Which it was. A world in which Grace had always been able to find joy. Happiness. Refuge from her own heartbreak. Working as a midwife in the maternity unit of St Aelina's hadn't been just a job for her. It had been a way of life. She'd adopted this country and its people and given them her heart. Before meeting Diego she'd thought she'd never leave the hospital in London. Never leave her country except for holidays. But Spain— Barcelona, St Aelina's—had become home. More than she'd ever thought possible.

The people, the weather, the historic beautiful buildings, the language… They had all made their way into her heart just as Diego had left it.

No. That wasn't true. He was still in her heart. He was her husband and, no matter what had happened between them, he would always have a place in her heart. Especially because of all that they had gone through. But she hadn't been able to keep him. He had walked away. Had not fought for them the way she'd hoped he would. And if he didn't want to fight...? Well, then. What was the point?

But as she stood there, looking at the hospital she'd thought she'd work in for the rest of her days, she knew she would have to tell her boss that she couldn't stay any more. That with her marriage over, with the way her life had crumbled, this place that had once given her such joy could only now cause her pain, if she stayed.

But she had more self-respect than that. She wouldn't linger in the hope that Diego would offer some small crumb of comfort, like friendship. That would be pathetic. It was love, or nothing, and he'd made it quite clear that he couldn't love her in the way she needed him to.

No. It was best to make a clean break.

Squaring her shoulders, she walked inside, ready to say hello to the many friends she hadn't seen for two weeks.

'Buenas noches.'

She said good evening to the night cleaners, the porters. She waved at Jorge, who ran the hospital café, as he left to get a good night's sleep.

Working the night shift was perfect for Grace. She had been unable to sleep for so long now that she might as well be working anyway. And, to be honest, it took her mind off her own problems. In every ward, every room of this hospital, stories were being played out. Some ended. Some became difficult roads to travel. But in Maternity new adventures began.

Families expanded. Miracles happened. People experienced joy and happiness and love such as they had never experienced before. Hearts expanded. Grew. Enveloped new faces and new lives. Sometimes there was grief. Sometimes there was pain and loss and despair. and Grace felt those keenly, tried vainly not to let them destroy her, considering her own past, but happiness outweighed those moments, and the thing about joy and happiness was that it was catching. All those in the department—the midwives, the doctors, the care assistants—got to share in a piece of those miracles. The IVF babies. The rainbow babies. The twins and triplets and multiples.

It was a special place to be.

She climbed the stairs to the first-floor maternity wing, rather than take the lift and risk running into Diego. He worked nights, too, but hopefully she wouldn't run into him just yet. Diego was a neonatal surgeon and worked on the second floor. Technically, she could get through a whole shift without seeing him if he wasn't needed. She hoped he wouldn't be. Crossed her fingers that all her mothers-to-be sailed through as normal, full-term cases.

Was she ready?

Could she ever be?

They would meet at some point, but she wanted a dose of happiness first, and so she greeted her friends and colleagues, and listened in to the hand-over, and then went to find her first labouring mother, who she was extremely pleased to discover would not need a neonatologist.

Alejandra de Leon was at term, fully dilated, and waiting for the urge to push. This was her first child with her husband Matteo, and up until this point she'd been cared for by Grace's friend and colleague Nena.

Grace introduced herself to Alejandra and Matteo. He looked excited and nervous as he set up cameras and recording devices from different viewpoints around the room—including one attached to the bedframe near his wife's head.

'Don't want to miss any of it?' she asked in Spanish, amused.

'We have a video channel.'

'You do?'

'Nearly a hundred thousand subscribers,' he said proudly.

'Wow. Your views are about to go way up, aren't they? Do you know what you're having? Did you do a gender reveal?'

'It's a surprise.' said Alejandra, rubbing her abdomen. 'Oh, another one's coming... should I push?'

Grace nodded. 'Take a deep breath and bear down, like you're having a bowel movement.'

She began coaching her. It was difficult sometimes for first-time mothers to know how to push. Some were afraid. Which was understandable. But that was why Grace was there. To encourage. To help. To motivate.

She wanted to see those babies born just as much as the parents did. There was nothing quite like that moment when the baby emerged, was draped on its mum's tummy and let out that first cry…

Matteo clutched his wife's hand, whispering words of encouragement. 'You're doing brilliantly. I love you. I love you so much!'

Alejandra turned and smiled and kissed him, but it wasn't long before another contraction began.

Grace counted to ten. She could see the baby's head. It had a lot of thick dark hair. 'Alejandra? Reach down and touch. The head's right there.'

She reached down. 'Oh!' She turned to look at her husband, her face a mix of surprise, love and awe.

Matteo kissed her on the forehead. 'You can do this! You good?'

Alejandra nodded and began to bear down with her next contraction. With each contraction that came the head emerged a little more, disappearing again as each pain ended.

'This is the hard part, but you can do it!' Grace told her. She didn't think that Alejandra needed an episiotomy—a small cut to help the baby pass through. And she'd only been pushing for about half an hour, so actually she was doing really well. And this was just what Grace needed. A straightforward birth. She had missed this.

Getting away for a couple of weeks and visiting Aunt Felicity had been wonderful, even if she had gone alone, her marriage in tatters. They'd had so many lovely walks along the beach, and hot chocolates in cafés, and fish and chips out of paper bags as they'd sat shivering on the blustery seafront, the British weather not providing them with the expected sunny weather despite it being July.

It had been great to see her aunt again, even though there'd been questions. Difficult questions. About what her future held. What decisions she needed to make. And about all the things she yearned for—like a baby of her own.

Not all her aunt's questions had had definitive answers, and a lot of the time all Grace kept hearing herself say was, *I don't know.*

Even when she'd come back to their home, here in Spain, she'd not found any answers. Just an empty flat. Lifeless. A pile of post on the mat. Nothing much in it except for a wedding invitation. Javier and Caitlin, their colleagues and friends, were getting married on the estate at Maravilla. The invitation should have made her happy, but it had just reinforced the fact that she had no idea if she would be attending that wedding. No idea at all. And what would she say to them if she saw them at the hospital? Because they'd expect her to say she'd be coming. With Diego.

It was all too much. Too complicated.

But *this* couple were about to become a family. Their lives were changing for evermore. Alejandra and Matteo were going to experience the one thing that Grace had yearned for, for years. She'd had no problem with getting pregnant. It was just the *staying* pregnant part that had eluded her.

But she refused to focus on that pain again. This wasn't about her. It was about this couple.

Alejandra screamed with the force of her latest contraction. *'Duele!' It hurts*.

'I know it does…it's just the baby's head, stretching everything. One more push and your baby's head will be out!'

Alejandra nodded and took a sip of water from the cup that Matteo held to her mouth.

He grabbed a facecloth and dabbed at her forehead. 'You're beautiful. I love you so much!'

Grace smiled at them both. It was so lovely to see it almost made her ache. She and Diego had been that much in love once. How had it gone so wrong?

Alejandra began to bear down again.

'That's it! Exactly right. Push harder! Harder! Okay, pant…'

The baby's head emerged, turning to face its mother's right thigh.

'Head's out! One last contraction, Alejandra, and you'll have your baby in your arms.'

Alejandra gasped, nodded, and squeezed her eyes shut as she pushed.

The shoulders emerged and Grace supported the baby. 'Open your eyes, Mummy, and reach down.'

She helped place the baby on her mother's stomach. Alejandra was crying with gratitude and relief, and Matteo's eyes wet with tears as the baby cried out. Suddenly everyone was laughing and cheering as Grace let Matteo cut the cord and draped a small blue towel around the baby.

Alejandra held her baby and cried happy tears.

'Want to see what you've had?' Grace asked.

Matteo reached forward, his hand gentle, as if touching the baby would somehow break it, his already radiant face breaking out into a bigger smile when he declared to his wife, 'It's a girl!'

Grace smiled for them both as she awaited the delivery of the placenta. Alejandra had only a small tear, and it was something that would heal on its own—she didn't need sutures. 'Have you chosen a name?'

'Eliana Maria.'

'That's a beautiful name. Happy birthday, Eliana.'

Grace checked the placenta, which was all fine, and the mum's blood loss was normal. Now was the time when she'd clean up, as unobtrusively as she could, so that this new family could have some privacy for a short time, before coming back to carry out the postnatal checks and Apgar score.

She wondered, as she always did at this moment, looking down on such a happy new family, if *she'd* ever get to experience this for herself. They looked so ecstatic in their little joyous bubble. Mum cradling baby in her arms... Dad half perched on the bed, his arm around his wife. Now that Eliana was here it was as if Grace wasn't even in the room any more.

'I'll be back in a few minutes.'

She backed away to the door. As much as Grace loved it when a baby was born, and everyone's faces erupted into smiles, she hated *this* moment. When she was forgotten, and yet again came the stark reminder that this happiness was not hers and she was not part of this family. They might remember her in the future, when they told the story of their child's birth. They might mention the lovely midwife who'd helped them get through it all, but that was all.

Grace silently closed the door behind her and let out a breath. As always, she felt the white-hot pain of her own empty arms, but she forced back the tears threatening to fall and headed to the board to update it, sniffing determinedly as she wrote up Alejandra's details. Next she stood up and went to the small kitchenette, knowing that Alejandra and Matteo would probably appreciate a nice cup of coffee each.

She poured the drinks into a couple of mugs and was just walking down to Alejandra's room when in her peripheral vision she caught movement off to her left. She glanced over with a smile, expecting to see Ana or Gabbi or Mira.

Only it wasn't.

Grace froze as her gaze met her husband's. *Diego.*

Her smile, meant for one of her colleagues, faltered as he stared back at her. She felt sick as her mouth dried out and her heart pounded furiously behind her ribcage. Why was he here? Who had called him down to this floor? She'd not heard of any early la-bourers in the hand-over when she'd arrived and she'd thought she'd have more time be-fore she saw him. Time so that she could mi-cromanage their first meeting, so that she'd be prepared, so that she'd know what to say and how to act. But to be caught off-guard like this…

He looked good—but of course he did. He was Diego! And apart from being tall and ripped and disturbingly sexy, the man saved babies' lives. Premature babies' lives. What *wasn't* there to drool over? Even from this distance his dark brown eyes bored into hers with an intensity that ought to come with a blood pressure warning, and he looked like he was growing a beard. The dark, stubble emphasising his jawline.

He wasn't smiling. In fact, he looked shocked to see her there. Just as unprepared as she was. And that made her feel a little bit better—because she'd been fighting to get some reaction out of him before he left and now she had one.

'Diego…'

She saw him swallow. Saw him look down at the blue file in his hand for an interminably long time. And then he turned and walked away without saying a word.

The second he was out of sight she realised how much she'd been sweating, how much tension she'd held in her chest and stomach and legs. Now it was as if she'd become boneless and weak, and she needed to sag against the wall for a moment, just to catch her breath and to stop the tears. Because, despite everything that they had gone through, she'd hoped that somehow, no matter how unexpected their meeting, that he would at least have said hello. That he might even have looked happy to see that she was back. Maybe even smiled. Only he hadn't.

He didn't even say hi.

Was she not worthy of acknowledgement?

Not even a nod of the head? Did he hate her so much that he couldn't even bear to look at her? That he'd walk away without saying a word? She knew that the last time they'd been together she'd stormed away from him and slammed the bedroom door, but... Surely they could be adult about this? They were going to have to work together, and they didn't need to transform this place, this hospital which had so very quickly become like home, into a place where she felt uncomfortable. Where their colleagues had to tread on eggshells around them. Where— God forbid—their friends felt they had to take sides.

It's a good thing, then, that I'm going to be leaving.

Grace squared her shoulders, stood up straight and rapped her knuckles gently on Alejandra and Matteo's door before going in with their coffees. She placed the drinks on a side cabinet and smiled at them. 'I just need to perform some newborn baby checks on Eliana and then I'll have her right back with you, okay?'

Alejandra nodded and placed the baby in Grace's arms. She looked down at the chubby little baby, admiring her thick dark hair, clenched tight fists and tiny button nose, and then laid her down in a bassinet.

One day she might be lucky enough to be a mother, but she very much doubted that it would happen any time soon. And it certainly wouldn't happen whilst she stayed married to Diego.

He clearly wanted nothing to do with her.

The sooner she went back home to Cornwall, the better.

Her marriage was over.

He'd been working non-stop whilst she was away—that was what he blamed it on. Being blindsided by the sight of his wife, back at work in St Aelina's. He'd been so busy bringing some medical notes down for tomorrow's day shift that he'd not even thought to remember that today was the night shift when Grace was due back.

And she'd looked...beautiful. She'd always had the power to grab his attention. The warm caramel of her hair had been twisted up into a bun, loose tendrils framing her heart-shaped face. And those startlingly blue eyes of hers—not pale, but richly blue, like the domed roofs in Santorini. To be caught in their gaze just now...

These last two weeks had been interminable. They were meant to have gone away together, to Cornwall, to visit her aunt. He liked Felicity. Loved her little seaside cottage. Liked the people there. They'd all made him so welcome—though her aunt hadn't been too impressed that she'd not been invited to their wedding.

He and Grace had married in London— a civil ceremony, near work, with two colleagues as witnesses. Not the big white beach wedding he'd later learned that Grace had always dreamed of, but they'd been so keen to get married. Grace had yearned to travel back to Barcelona with him, settle down and begin a family together. At the time it had seemed time was ticking away too fast, and their love for one another had been so all-consuming it had seemed the right thing to do. Just get married as fast as they could, leave London, come to Spain, then have fun trying to start that family.

The world had been at their feet and they'd thought anything was possible.

Now look at us.

It had hurt to see her. Physically hurt. As if someone had pounded him in the chest and then his gut, just to doubly make sure that he was winded enough to be unable to speak. His gaze had caught in hers and it had been like being caught in a beam of light… just like in those sci-fi shows he loved so much. Unable to move. Unable to breathe. Unable to *think*.

He'd wanted more than anything to run to her, to pull her into his embrace and hold her tight and never let her go. To say sorry over and over again. They'd only been apart these last two weeks, but before that they'd argued so badly and he'd moved out, feeling he had no other choice.

Since bringing her here to his home in Barcelona all he had caused her was pain. Grief. Loss. Upset. Heartbreak. Their hopes and dreams had been destroyed.

He'd wanted to run to her. Wanted to hold her in his arms. To say sorry. But the shock of seeing her… He'd clenched his jaw, looked down at the paperwork in his hands as if to remind himself of why he was there, and then, grounding himself somehow, he had found the strength to walk away from his wife.

He told himself he would talk to her later. Maybe he would find the right words then? Maybe in the future they would be able to talk without causing each other upset? Perhaps time would heal all wounds, as people said it did. That was what they needed. More time.

But for now those things didn't seem possible. And each step that took him further and further away from her orbit just made him heartsick. Just like when he'd packed his things a few weeks ago. He'd hated doing so. Almost hadn't been able to believe he was! But he'd done it for her. She didn't understand. Hadn't understood his silence or why he'd not said anything.

Maybe she would never understand that.

For now, though, he could soften the blow, knowing that she was back. They'd have time to sort through their problems. There would be no more breaks. No more going away. It might take a few weeks, or maybe even months, but they would be able to talk again.

But for now it's for the best. For both of us.

Grace had just finished escorting Alejandra and baby Eliana to the postnatal ward when her pager sounded. She checked the display and saw that she was urgently needed down in the ER.

She dialled from the midwives' station. 'I've been paged?'

'We've an urgent case coming in and you've been requested by name.'

That was odd. 'Who by?'

'The paramedic.'

The only paramedic who really knew her name was Isabella. *Diego's older sister.*

'I'll be right down. Do we know who they're bringing in?'

'We've only got vague details. But it's a young female in premature labour.'

Oh.

Grace was used to being called down to the ER. The midwives were often paged to consult on a woman who was in labour. But if *Isabella* was bringing someone in... If her sister-in-law had time, would she want to take her to one side and talk about what was happening between Grace and her brother? Did she even know? Would she say something to her? And if this was a preemie then that would mean they would also need the help of a neonatologist at some point, and the only one she'd seen on the night shift, too, was her husband.

Diego.

The two of them.

Together.

That's going to be awkward.

She almost—*almost*—considered getting one of the others to go and meet the ambulance. But Grace had never been a coward—and anyway, maybe Issy would be rushed off her feet and unable to stay once she'd dropped off her patient. And maybe, if the gods were kind, this young lady might not even be in premature labour at all. Her dates could be wrong.

Maybe.

Am I ever that lucky?

She didn't want to think about the answer to that much.

'I'll be right down.'

Grace replaced the receiver of the phone and stared at it, her stomach churning slightly. She looked up as Ana approached. 'I've got to head down to the ER. Possible preemie. Can you alert upstairs for me? Check they've got a spare incubator?'

'Sure.' Ana smiled.

Grace headed to the lifts and bypassed them, opening the door to the stairs and trotting down them, her mind awhirl with possibilities. What if Isabella had heard about Diego moving out? What if her sister-in-law was angry with her? Isabella and Diego didn't seem all that close, but would that matter? She wasn't sure she'd be able to stand up to a fiery Spaniard right now.

When she made it to the ER, she saw Issy wheeling her patient into cubicle three. The patient looked as if she was in pain.

Grace smiled, hesitant. 'Hi. What have we got?'

'This is Zara. She's eighteen years old, complaining of abdominal pains that come and go, and estimates that she's about eight months pregnant.'

Grace looked at Issy. 'Estimates?'

'She's been living on the streets. No scans. No healthcare.' Isabella sounded concerned. As if she couldn't quite believe it. 'She doesn't even know how many babies are in there.'

Right.

'Hi, Zara. My name's Grace,' she said in Spanish. 'I'm a midwife and I'm going to be looking after you.' She smiled, before turning back to Isabella. 'Where did you find her?'

'In St Aelina's Park. She's been sleeping in the folly.'

Poor girl. 'Okay, Zara, tell me about these abdominal pains. Can you describe them for me?'

Zara began to give a description, but it didn't sound like labour to Grace.

'Can I have a feel of your tummy?'

Zara nodded.

'I'll leave you to it.' said Isabella, almost sharply.

Grace turned to thank her, expecting a glare, or something, but her sister-in-law didn't even look at her. She seemed distracted. As if she just wanted to get out of the ER as quickly as possible.

Grace watched her go, pushing away the trolley that they'd wheeled Zara in on. It was weird, but Grace was thankful. Isabella hadn't said a word about her and Diego! Perhaps she didn't know that they'd split up yet.

She concentrated on palpating Zara's abdomen, then used her tape to measure the height of the fundus—the top part of the womb. Thirty-six centimetres. 'You're right. You're nearly full-term and baby is head-down, which is good. I'm going to put you on a trace machine, if that's okay? It will allow us to monitor the baby's heartbeat and check for contractions.'

Zara nodded.

She was eighteen. She must be terrified.

'Anyone we can call for you? Friends? Family?' Grace couldn't imagine being this young and this pregnant, in pain and alone.

This time Zara shook her head and looked away from her.

'What about the baby's father?'

Another head-shake, and this time the welling of tears.

Grace's heart ached for the young girl and she placed a hand on Zara's arm. 'That's all right. You're safe now. I'm going to look after you, okay?'

Zara nodded.

'To make sure I can do that properly, I need to gather some information. I'll need to take some blood from you and ask you about your medical history. Is that all right?'

'I guess…'

'And maybe get you to do a wee sample, too?'

Again, the girl nodded.

'One last question?'

Zara looked at her, uncertain. Almost angry 'What?'

Grace smiled. 'Would you like a drink?'

It was the first time she'd seen even the hint of a smile.

Whilst Zara was having a scan, Grace took the opportunity to create a new patient record for her on the computer. They were on a maternity ward now. It seemed a better place for Zara to be—away from the chaos and noise of the ER. The emergency room could be a frightening place, and Zara was already scared.

Grace couldn't imagine being in the young girl's position. Eighteen and pregnant and living on the street. It was no place to be—not for anyone. And yet she still found herself envying the young girl, because despite her situation Zara was about to do something that Grace had been unable to achieve—she was about to become a mother.

Life very often played games like that, Grace thought. There were many people in the world like her—hard-working, honest, kind. People who had a decent home, who were law-abiding, who had never done anything wrong in their lives. And some of them were desperate to start a family and couldn't. Either the women couldn't get pregnant at all, or they were couples like Grace and Diego. The women could get pregnant, but they lost their babies—every single time.

And then there were other kinds of people. The women who abused their bodies for years with alcohol or drugs, or committed crimes, did terrible things. And they seemed to get pregnant at the drop of a hat. Grace wasn't saying that they didn't deserve to be parents…just that it seemed unfair. Sometimes you could do everything right in life and yet…

Poor Zara. What had happened to her? Where were her family? She must have some—somewhere. Even if she'd have to go and live with an aunt, the way Grace had when she'd lost her parents.

It had happened when she was so young. Grace's parents had been crazy in love and had wanted to live life to the full by travelling around the world. And yet their promise, their lives, had been cut short by a tragic car accident that had killed them both almost instantly. That was when Grace had been taken in by Aunt Felicity. Dear, quiet, reserved Aunt Felicity, who'd worked as a nurse and inspired Grace to join the medical profession, thrilled to discover her niece wanted to train as a midwife.

And although Grace had missed out on having a large family, living in a home filled with noise and laughter, she'd always thought she could build one of her own by marrying a man she fell in love with and having plenty of babies.

But she'd not been able to do even that simple task.

She'd fallen in love. She'd found the man. She'd got pregnant. And then her body had failed her. Time after time after time. And with each loss her husband had spent more and more time away from her. Almost as if he couldn't bear to be with her.

He'd clearly thought he'd made a terrible mistake. Because Diego came from a huge family. Six siblings! Isabella was the oldest, then Diego, then Eduardo, Frida, Luis and Paola. All grown-up now, but Diego had lain in her arms when she was pregnant with their first child and told her that he would love to have lots of babies with her. That he wanted the kind of big family that he was used to. And she had laughed with him, agreed with him, and told him that she wanted that too. That she would have as many of his babies as she could.

Grace let out a sigh, not wanting to dwell on her pain and grief, and luckily she didn't have to as Zara was wheeled back to the ward. Grace gave her a little wave from the desk, and then got up to go and talk to her patient.

'I've got some of your results back. The pains you were having earlier…you have a urinary tract infection. They can happen to anybody, so I don't want you worrying about that. We'll start you on a course of antibiotics and keep you here, so we can maintain your hydration and feed you up a bit before you go into labour fully.'

'My baby is all right?'

'I'm just waiting for your scan results to come through, but you've been feeling the baby kick and move?'

Zara nodded.

'Then those are good signs. Let's start you on the antibiotics and wait for your scan result. One thing at a time, okay?'

'Okay. Thank you.'

Grace stroked her arm. 'No problem. I'll leave you to get settled, but I'll be right outside if you need anything. Press this button here, okay?' She passed Zara the patient remote control and then headed back to the desk. But suddenly right there—right in front of her—was her husband. Diego. Her gaze locked with his and her breath caught in her throat. She swallowed hard.

He looked past her with regret, and his gaze was full of apology as he locked eyes with Zara. 'I have your scan results.'

CHAPTER TWO

GRACE.

He'd not expected her to be right there! She was so close to him. Close enough to reach out and touch. And by God he wanted to! But he couldn't do that any more, seeing as he'd walked away—and besides, he was here to give Zara the results of her scan. He was here for the patient and her baby— not, unfortunately, for Grace. He knew they needed to talk, but he couldn't imagine that that would be easy.

Nor was the news that he was about to deliver to Grace's patient.

'My name is Dr Diego Rivas. I'm a neonatal surgeon and I'll be in charge of your case.'

He saw Zara glance at Grace, and watched as Grace went to her and took hold of her hand.

'It's okay. Just listen.'

Grace was smiling at Zara. Her smile telling Zara that she could trust him. Clearly they had developed a bond. He and Grace had once had a bond, but now that was a broken and ragged thing. Torn. Weak. In tatters.

'We noticed during the scan that the level of your amniotic fluid is quite low, but also that your baby has a condition called exomphalos.' Diego risked a quick glance at Grace. She would know what that was, and what exactly Zara would be facing over the next few weeks.

Grace squeezed Zara's hand.

'What the hell is that?' Zara asked, her voice full of fear and panic.

He was about to answer, but Grace got there first.

'It means that as your baby developed in your womb, the baby's intestines didn't relocate as they should have from the umbilical cord, so remain in a sac outside of the abdomen.'

'Ay, Dios mio!' Zara swung her legs off the bed. 'No. No, I'm not doing this! Let me go!'

Diego took a few steps back. He could tell this young girl was incredibly frightened. 'Please,' he said in a low, urgent voice. 'We need you to stay.'

Zara glanced at Grace.

'Your baby needs looking after. You need to stay here,' she told her.

'Did I do this?' Zara asked. 'Because I didn't get checked?'

She was like a cornered animal. Glancing from Grace to Diego and back again. He felt she might bolt at any moment unless they played this right, and he couldn't afford for that to happen. Because if this young girl went into labour on the streets with a baby with exomphalos… Well, it wouldn't have a great ending.

Diego shook his head. 'No. No one knows what causes this to happen. But we know about it now and we can be prepared for it when he's born.'

Zara stared at him. 'He?'

He smiled and nodded.

'He. A little boy.' That seemed to really sink in. Made Zara think.

Diego glanced at his wife. They needed to persuade this young girl to stay. 'We'll need to perform a more detailed scan, so we'd like to keep you in and I need to devise a plan for after he is born. He's going to need surgery to put his intestines back inside his abdominal cavity.'

Zara's eyes welled up with tears. 'Could he die?'

Diego paused. He hated this question. All parents wanted to hear that their baby would be fine, and he could never promise that. But if he didn't promise would she run?

'All surgeries carry risk, Zara. But he has a good chance here—better than if you were back on the street. And we will do our very best to get both him and you through this.'

'Will I have to have a caesarean?'

'No. You can give birth normally. But we would like to monitor you both closely.'

Zara crumpled and began to sob. Loud cries of pain and anguish. It was terrible to hear, and all he could do was reach for tissues and pass them to her, one hand rubbing her back as he tried to calm her and reassure her.

He was acutely aware that his wife was on the opposite side of Zara, doing the same thing, and he wanted nothing more than to look at her and acknowledge her help, or smile at her, or *something*. But Grace wasn't looking at him. Her full attention was on their patient.

Grace was smiling, whispering comforting words. 'We'll get you a private room, okay? But I need you to promise us that you'll stay here until both you and the baby are well?'

Zara sniffed, wiping her nose on her sleeve. She looked up at him, her gaze assessing, checking, trying to see if she could trust him. Then she glanced at Grace—who, he had to admit, was being amazing.

But then again, she always was.

Finally, Zara nodded. 'Fine. But I'm only going to deal with you two. No one else.'

He nodded. That was fine. It might give him the opportunity to smooth things over with Grace, too. 'Agreed.'

After Diego left the ward Grace let out a breath, releasing the strain she'd been under in his presence. She wasn't looking forward to having to work closely with him over the next few weeks, but she would do so for the sake of her patient, who she already felt a kinship with.

Zara had no one fighting for her. No one in her corner. At least, no one she knew about. So, in lieu of family, Grace was happy to do whatever was needed to get this girl and her baby good care. Something they would both need a lot of.

'When did you last eat something?' she asked.

Zara looked embarrassed. 'I can't remember. Yesterday? Maybe...'

She nodded. 'I'll see what I can rustle up. And I'll bring you a menu later, so you can order your meals for tomorrow.'

'Thank you.'

Grace smiled. 'It's no problem. And I'll try and organise that private room for you—unless you'd like to stay on the ward? It's just that you'll see a lot of people come and go...it might be quite noisy for you, and you need to build yourself up and rest.'

'A room of my own?' Zara seemed to think about that. 'I've never had one.'

'Then let's find you one. I'll be back soon, okay?'

Zara nodded.

Grace headed out of the ward, squirting her hands with antibacterial gel and rubbing them together, hoping that the midwife in charge would agree to a private room. But as she approached the desk she could already see Diego talking to her, and assumed that he was arguing Zara's case for one. She didn't want to talk to him right now, so she walked past him and headed to the small kitchenette, to see if she could find a sand-wich, or something she could make for Zara.

She'd only been in there for a few min-utes when she heard the door open. When she turned, expecting to see one of the other midwives, the smile on her face froze, then disappeared when she saw Diego standing there.

Grace's heart began to thud, but she turned away from him and began making a sandwich, glad to have something for her hands to do.

'You're back.'

She wished her hands would stop shak-ing. It was hard to put butter on the bread and spread it evenly with him standing be-hind her.

'It's good to see you.'

Ham. Cheese. Salad. Maybe a yoghurt? Grace tried to focus on Zara's food. Tried to ignore her husband behind her.

And then he said, 'I missed you.'

He was kidding, right? After everything that had happened. After letting her get so wound up that she'd ranted and raved, hop-ing that he would tell her that they still had something to fight for.

Grace turned and looked at him incredulously. 'Are you kidding me?' She pointed at him with the butter knife.

'I just thought that—'

'No! You don't get to think *anything*, Diego!' She threw the knife down into the sink and leaned against it, breathing heavily, trying to calm herself, trying to keep her voice down. Their colleagues and patients didn't need to hear them arguing. 'You moved out. You left. You ignored me in corridors. You hardly spoke to me for weeks. Avoided me. And now, when I've been away for two weeks, you have the audacity to tell me that you've *missed* me?' She laughed. '*You* made the choice to leave. Mentally, emotionally and physically. Do you know what that did to me? At all?'

He stared back at her.

'Those weeks in Cornwall were hell for me, knowing my marriage was over. *Over!* I've spent the last two weeks getting used to that fact and telling myself that there's nothing between us any more, and now, when I come back to work, you tell me you've missed me? What? Do you think I'm some sort of plaything that you can toy with? Do you enjoy torturing me? Is that it?'

'Of course not,' he said quietly, looking suitably apologetic.

'Then don't say things like that to me. We talk about work. Nothing else. We talk about that young girl who's depending on both of us? We need to be professional for her sake. I will work with you, and I will be polite and considerate, but all I can be to you right now is your colleague and nothing else. Because I need to work on mending the heart that *you broke*. And you telling me that you miss me...? That just opens up old wounds.'

She stared hard at him. Hoping and praying that he would understand, that he wouldn't push for more. Not that she thought he would. He was probably keen to know where they stood with each other, too. Keen to hear that she didn't expect anything of him. Because he had made his choice clear.

'I'm sorry, and of course I shall abide by your wishes.'

She'd expected that. But to actually hear him agree with her that it was over... That hurt all over again. Some small part of her must have still wanted to hear him say *It's not over. Not yet. I love you. Let's fight for us*. Only he didn't. He agreed with her.

She turned away to hide her tears, angrily

grabbing another knife from the drawer and cutting up the sandwich, placing it on a plate and then pushing past him and heading towards Zara's room.

Grace couldn't mend them, but she could help Zara. And this place—St Aelina's maternity unit—had always brought her calm and happiness. Even on the worst days.

She needed it to work its magic once again.

The hospital rooftop had always been a haven for Diego. It wasn't pretty, by any means. Air-conditioning vents, chimneys, wires—it was all very industrial. But it had become a place for him to think. A sanctuary that only he seemed to know about or access. From here he could look out to the blue sea, focus on the horizon and take a few deep, steadying breaths. Sometimes, if he couldn't make it all the way to the beach, he would stand here and watch the sun rise.

He'd come here whenever there had been a Covid surge. Every break that he could manage he'd come up here—just to take the mask off his face and breathe. To steady his nerves, to gird himself for the battle that was being waged below, in almost every

room, of life over death. Too often they'd
lost that battle, and he'd lost count of the
number of times he'd had to ring a family
member to tell them of a loss. And each loss
had been another stab to the heart. As if
it was personal. Despite their vast knowledge, their years of training, their science,
their medicines, they were losing the battle.
Each death had told Diego that they weren't
good enough. They weren't clever enough.

They simply weren't *enough*.

He wasn't enough.

As always, his thoughts drifted to the joy
he had experienced at discovering Grace
was pregnant. A smile crept across his face
as he remembered how happy she'd been
to tell him! He could see her face now. The
brightness of her eyes. The wideness of her
smile. They'd both wanted to start a family.
They'd both dreamed of having a big one—a
house filled with love and laughter and joy.

And then she'd lost the baby. Just a few
weeks after discovering she was pregnant.
Grace had lain curled up in bed, her face
drawn and pale, her cheeks tear-stained, crying for hours until the bleeding had stopped.

He'd done what he could. Tried to reassure
her that these things often happened with

first pregnancies. That it had never been meant to be. That there must have been a developmental abnormality or something like that. He'd spoken to her like a medic to make her see that it wasn't her fault, that there was nothing either of them could have done, trying to be a calm port in a storm as she'd grieved for the baby she'd loved and lost.

He'd hurt, too. Of course he had. He'd had so many plans in his head. He'd wondered what type of father he would be. Thought of the games he would play. The bonding moments with his son or daughter. To lose that possibility...to lose that wish had been devastating. All he'd wanted to do was curl into a ball himself and grieve for the child that would never be born. Never have a name.

But his wife hadn't needed him to be falling apart when she was, and he'd wanted back the woman he loved, and so he'd been her shoulder to cry on. Her listening ear. The rock that she'd needed. Swallowing down his own pain to deal with hers.

Eventually they'd decided to try again, when she'd felt ready, and they'd allowed the hope and the excitement of trying to conceive to fill their lives with joy and laughter as Grace had quickly fallen pregnant a second time.

They'd both been thrilled, and optimistically cautious, and when Grace had made it past the first trimester they'd gone out and finally told everyone. Their colleagues. Their friends. Isabella. The rest of his siblings. Aunt Felicity. With each new person they'd told it had made the reality of the baby even more official. The world had finally seemed back on its axis once again, and at the first scan they'd both cried to see the baby's heart beating so fast and so strong!

They'd begun making plans. Grace had bought some maternity outfits. They'd begun working on the spare room to make it into a nursery. Having conversations about paint colours. Names. Feeling nothing could go wrong this time. They'd had their bad luck.

So when tragedy had struck a second time, six months in, and Grace had had to give birth to a stillborn baby, they had been broken. Torn apart. His stoicism and wise words had meant nothing to her and she'd lashed out in her grief and anger at the world.

He'd tried. He'd really tried to be there for her. But her pain had been such that he hadn't been able to handle seeing her broken that way. When he had tried to comfort her it had done nothing, and so he'd begun to look for excuses to stay at work, knowing he shouldn't, but also knowing he needed time for himself, to grieve in private.

He would never forget what it had felt like to look down at his stillborn son. They'd taken a long time to heal from that second loss. Their relationship had not the same feel as before Grace had tried to get pregnant. Their freedom, their happiness at life in general being good, was gone. They'd both been tempered by loss. They'd sniped at one another without thinking. They'd felt wary of ever trying again. They'd been nervous. Anxious even to suggest it—even though it was all they could think about…having a child.

When she'd got pregnant a third time, unexpectedly, neither of them had felt happy. Neither of them had been carefree. Grace had panicked over every twinge. Every symptom. His wife had changed from the woman she'd once been to a woman who was nervous, fidgety, who chewed on her lip constantly, who kept going to the toilet to look for blood, who barely wanted to move, just in case…

They made it to the thirteen-week scan.

But the baby had not.

The third loss was the thing that had totally destroyed them.

He'd had no words for her. Nothing at all. And she'd just seemed so lost in her own pain and grief that she'd hardly noticed that he was grieving too. With nothing to say to her he'd stayed at work, taking on extra shifts, giving his all to his patients because his wife wouldn't let him take care of her.

His patients had salved his pain somewhat. Here at St Aelina's he could help. He could make a difference. He could be the puppet master for happy outcomes. They weren't his, exactly, but he felt triumph with every baby he saved. Every baby he saw go home the way his own babies never had.

Here on the rooftop he could breathe.

Here on the rooftop he could tell himself that what he did mattered.

Here on the rooftop he could tell himself that somehow, someday, he and Grace might work things out.

Zara lay on the bed, about to have a more detailed scan of her baby. Grace sat to one side of her, holding her hand, whilst Diego performed the ultrasound himself. They already knew this baby had exomphalos, but he knew that babies with that condition often had comorbidities—other conditions alongside it—and he wanted to be informed before the baby was born.

Pre-warned was pre-armed.

This second scan would give them that knowledge and allow them to be ready for when the baby arrived, and if it needed emergency surgery straight after it was born, to ensure its survival, then so be it.

'The gel might feel a little cold,' he said.

He placed the transducer onto her abdomen and began to move it around to get the basic picture of how the baby was lying, before he could look for more markers.

'What exactly are you looking for?' asked Zara. 'You already know what's wrong with him.'

'We're just checking to make sure there's nothing else. Dr Rivas will also get a chance to have a more detailed look at the exomphalos, as he will be operating,' Grace said in a soft, low voice.

It was the one she used so as not to frighten her patients. He'd heard her use it before. But this was the first time he'd heard her refer to him as *Dr Rivas*. What? Couldn't she even call him Diego any more? Was this her way of trying to create distance between them?

He'd had plenty of time to stew on his decision to move out, to walk away, and for most of the time he believed he'd made the right choice. It had become unbearable to witness his wife's pain whilst trying to work through his own privately. But in moments like this, when she couldn't even refer to him by his first name, he began to see the extra damage he might have caused her.

And he'd never wanted to do that.

The exomphalos was sizeable. In the pouch he could see the intestines, and a small portion of the baby's liver. A silo pouch would be the best option for reduction, he thought, as he moved the transducer to look for any other abnormalities. He began at the head and moved down, then paused, hovering around the throat and upper chest area.

'What is it?' Zara asked. 'What's wrong now?'

He zoomed in, tried to see more clearly. 'I think I can see an atresia.'

'What's that?'

He could hear the panic in her voice.

'An atresia is a condition in which a passage or orifice in the body is closed or completely absent,' Grace said calmly.

'It looks like an oesophageal atresia, Zara,' he confirmed, moving the transducer this way and that to get a proper look. 'The oesophagus is your baby's food pipe. If it is indeed closed, and it looks like it is, it means your baby won't be able to feed normally. The milk won't make it to baby's stomach.'

'Oh, my God!' Zara began to cry. 'Does that mean he's going to die if he can't eat?'

He shook his head. 'No, no. Not at all. We can perform surgery to reconnect the two pouch ends. It looks like your baby has developed a tracheoesophageal fistula. That sounds scary, but what it means is that when your baby was developing the body created an abnormal junction. We can sort this out with surgery after he's born, at the same time as we work on his exomphalos.'

But Zara was crying heavily now. 'Is it my fault? It's my fault, isn't it?'

'Hey, now, no…it's not your fault. No one knows what causes these things to happen. They just do.' Grace stood and grasped Zara's hand more tightly and made the young girl look at her. 'Listen to me. We know now. We can help him. We can do this.'

Grace was so good with patients. It was what had initially made him fall in love with her. She just got it. She knew how to relate to them. She knew how scared they could be and she knew the right words and the right tone to use. She gave them strength. Strength they'd never known they had. When a woman in the final stages of labour felt she had nothing left to give, no more strength to push, Grace could help her dig down deep and find it.

He wished he could have done the same for her when she'd needed strength.

Guilt flooded him and he looked away, unable to bear witness any more. He focused on checking the rest of Zara's baby. He clenched his jaw and concentrated hard on the scan images, remembering to print a couple off so Zara could look at them.

'We're all done. I couldn't see anything else.'

Grace didn't look at him. She just looked at her patient. 'That's great news. All you need to focus on now, Zara, is growing your little boy so he comes out big and strong and ready for his surgery.'

'Promise me he won't die.'

He looked at Grace again. They couldn't promise that.

'Everything will be just fine.' His wife smiled.

Zara was settled back in her private room, and Grace was about to go and check on another patient, when Diego stopped her in the corridor. She could see him standing there. Waiting for her. Hands on hips, looking incredibly fed up.

Sucking in a deep breath, she went to pass him, but he stepped in front of her. 'You shouldn't have told her that everything would be fine. You don't know that.'

'She needed to hear something positive. All you've done since getting on this case is give her bad news.'

'I told her the truth. She needs to know that.'

'And the truth of those surgeries is that they usually go well.'

'Usually. But you know that every surgery carries a risk, and we have no idea how Zara's baby will react to being under anaesthetic. There could be complications. She needed to hear the reality of the situation.'

'Which you're so good at delivering.' She

could feel anger and hurt rising over his criticism of how she was handling Zara's case. She pushed past him, rage flaring, and before she knew it turned to face him again. 'Would it hurt you to show some compassion? To stop being a doctor and for once—*just once*—show that you're a human being?'

Before he could answer, she pushed open her next patient's door and went inside, forcing a smile, knowing she had to leave her private feelings outside. Right now this couple, Carlita and Emilio, needed calm, confident vibes.

'How are we doing?' she asked.

Carlita was still only four centimetres dilated with her first baby, so she had a few hours to go yet.

Grace checked the trace of the baby's heartbeat and noted that Carlita seemed to be contracting every five to six minutes. Then she settled herself into a corner of the room and noted down other observations—temperature, blood pressure, blood sugar. Carlita was suffering from gestational diabetes and was being induced at thirty-seven weeks, because her baby was already registering at around nine pounds.

'You're doing great. How do you feel?'

Carlita smiled nervously. 'I'm okay so far. Nervous of what's to come.'

'That's understandable. But what you've got to remember is that no matter what happened to other women in labour, no matter what horror stories you might have been told by well-meaning friends and family, your labour and your birth will be your own experience. Some women sail through without making a sound. A couple of pushes and the baby is out. No one ever tells those stories, do they?'

She smiled, thinking back to when she'd lost her first baby. How so many women had told her that they'd also experienced a miscarriage the first time they'd got pregnant. That it was normal. Natural. And that they'd gone on to have four kids. Five. Twins. Triplets. It had seemed that everyone had a success story to tell her.

When she'd lost the second baby they'd had less to say. When she'd lost the third it had felt as if women looked at her differently. They'd hidden their own pregnancies, hadn't told her until they absolutely had to, thinking that she was going to get upset.

She *had* been upset. Of course she had! It had seemed all the women in the whole world could get pregnant and deliver safe, happy, healthy babies except for her. Coming into work each day had been painful. Each birth a stark reminder of what she had lost. What she and Diego were missing. But eventually these births had become comforting. Each baby in its mother's arms a victory.

Maybe they weren't hers, but she lived vicariously through them.

Grace had come to accept that she would never have children. Never have the large family that she'd always craved. Something was wrong with her. It was no wonder that Diego had left. He wanted a large family, too. He'd grown up in one. Five siblings! She couldn't even begin to imagine what that must have been like, having grown up an only child herself.

He'd tried to tell her once. Told her about how Isabella had looked after them all after their mother had passed away when baby Paola was only one year old. Isabella had been thirteen—much too young to take on such a responsibility—but as the eldest she had done so. And then his father had become ill a few years later, and she'd taken on more, becoming his carer too.

They'd all tried their best to be good, and

not cause her too much work, but there had been six of them and Isabella had lost her teenage years—Diego, too, as he'd become the man of the house. They'd tried to instil fun and laughter into their lives, but it had been hard, and as soon as they could they'd all flown the nest, spreading out across Spain, though he and Isabella both still lived in Barcelona.

Diego didn't seem all that close to his sister. They stayed out of each other's way, mostly, but Grace knew there must be love there. Appreciation.

Diego had looked for his freedom before.

Now he was free to find someone who could give him a family.

The thought saddened her. Made tears sting the backs of her eyes. She blinked them away rapidly. Maybe once she got back to the UK she should start divorce proceedings. There would be no point in hanging on to a relationship that had fizzled out, despite how strongly it had started.

Warmth spread through her at the thought of happier times long past. How she'd been working in that hospital in London and looked up at the sound of footsteps com-

ing down the long corridor and seen him—
Diego—for the first time.

Had it been love at first sight?

Lust at first sight?

All she knew was that her heart had begun
to pound, her mouth had gone dry, and she'd
felt like a silly teenage girl with an immediate crush. That hair, those beautiful dark
brown eyes, so full of exotic spirit. His gaze
had met hers and for just a moment time had
stood still and the rest of the world had faded
away. She'd been rushed off her feet at work.
The ward had been full of new mothers that
day. Grace had struggled to find time for a
decent break, and she'd felt exhausted, but
in that one moment as their eyes had met all
that had fallen away.

Tiredness—gone.

Aching legs—gone.

The desire for a cup of tea and a sit-down—
gone.

And then time had begun again, and he'd
smiled at her and nodded, and her cheeks
had flushed, and that had been that. Hook,
line and sinker. When he'd found her at the
end of his shift and asked her out of course
she'd said yes! Despite the fact that only
hours before all she'd wanted from her eve-

ning was to lie in the bath with a good book and have a soak before falling into bed.

Instead, she'd ended up dancing the night away in some club, with Diego teaching her how to salsa. And when they'd gone back to his home she'd ended up in his shower with him, and there had been no reading done, no standing there letting the spray from the water refresh her body.

Diego had done all that. And more. And afterwards they had fallen into bed and carried on enjoying and exploring each other.

She'd fallen hard and fast. They'd had a whirlwind romance and when Diego had proposed she'd thought nothing in the world could ever make her happier.

Where had all that excitement gone?

Where had the love gone?

Grace knew she should never have said what she had just now. Diego had actually been very good at explaining to Zara what would need to happen, and he'd been absolutely right that she shouldn't have told her that everything would be all right when she had no way of knowing for sure.

But it was just...

Whenever she'd needed him to say some encouraging words, or soothe her soul, he had always just stuck to the facts. Been clinical. Been Dr Rivas rather than Diego, her loving husband.

She'd wanted a sign that her loving husband was still there somewhere.

But all he continued to show her was that he was nowhere to be seen.

CHAPTER THREE

'GRACE? COULD I have a word with you before you go?'

Her supervisor and chief midwife, Renata, stood in the doorway to her office. Grace had been about to go home. To get some much-needed sleep, if she could, in the cold and empty apartment that had once felt like home.

'Sure.' She followed Renata into her office. 'What's up?'

'Olivia has been called away to Andalusia, to look after her mother who's had a stroke, so I'm going to be short on night staff for a while. Could you cover her night shifts for the next few weeks? I appreciate it's a pain, but you're the most senior midwife amongst everyone, and I need to know I have someone I can trust on nights.'

Oh. Grace hadn't been expecting this.

She'd been hoping to speak to Renata about giving her notice and leaving… But their patients meant more to her than any personal requirements right now—plus, that would allow her to follow through on Zara's baby. She had promised, after all.

'All right. That seems okay. Do we know how long Olivia might be in Andalusia?'

'Long enough for her to make sure her mum's okay. I think she wants to see her through the beginning of her physio and then get help arranged before she can come back.'

Grace nodded. 'Keep me informed.'

'I will. Did you have a nice break back home?'

She thought of her time in Cornwall. Alone. 'It was different. Cold.'

'Once you get used to the Spanish sun…' Renata smiled.

'Exactly.' She stood to go, said goodbye, and headed out of the hospital.

It had been a crazy first shift back. Running into Diego like that when she'd not expected it. Then his rather distracted sister. Realising she'd have to work with Diego on Zara, and now she was going to be on nights for a while. Maybe Diego would be on day shifts? Maybe he could keep an eye on Zara during the day, whilst she looked out for her at night? That seemed sensible. Perhaps she should suggest it to him. Tell him it was in their patient's best interests, rather than mention the fact that she didn't want to argue with him all the time and running into him each night would be incredibly distracting.

Night shifts were crazy. The hospital was a different world at night. It was more intimate. And did she want intimacy with Diego?

Physically, she missed him. He'd been gone from her bed for a long time now. She missed the feel of him in her arms. The way it had felt to wake in the morning and see him lying beside her, his face in soft repose. The way she would often lean over and touch him, watching his face, waiting for him to wake up and smile at her, reach for her, pull her close so they could lose themselves in each other.

She couldn't remember the last time they'd done that. She couldn't remember the last time they had laughed with one another. Couldn't remember the last time they had simply sat on the sofa, watching a movie, sharing a bowl of popcorn.

When had it gone so wrong?

After the first miscarriage? Or the second? Or the third? Or had it been when Diego had realised that her empty, barren womb would not give him what he wanted? When he'd realised that if he were to have the family he wanted he would have to find it elsewhere? When he'd begun to pull away from her and retreat into medicine? Into work? Taking extra shifts in a bid not to be near her? When she had started doing the same?

I'm hungry.

She hadn't eaten all night. She'd been with Zara and then with Carlita for most of it—Carlita having given birth to a bouncing baby boy just before Grace's shift had ended. It was always nice to leave on a high. But she'd been denied even that. The baby's blood sugar had been low and he'd been taken to the NICU as a precaution, until he could be stabilised.

Grace knew she had to think of her own blood sugar. As she walked through the streets she thought about going to La Casa. It was a nice little traditional Catalan breakfast place that she and Diego knew. A place they'd often gone to for breakfast after sharing a night shift. The idea of sinking her teeth into their delicious *torrada amb tomà-*

quet or their deliciously thick *punxo de truita* made her mouth water. The owner, Felipe, knew exactly how she liked it.

But the idea of walking into La Casa alone, sitting at a table by the window alone, forcing a smile for Felipe, pretending that everything was all right, facing his questions…

No. I can't do it.

Instead, she allowed herself to enter a fast-food joint that was open twenty-four hours and picked up a hot chocolate and a rather lacklustre breakfast sandwich that was thin and simply filled a hole.

The owner there didn't know her name. The staff didn't know her or greet her or say goodbye. They simply moved on to the next customer. It was almost as if she wasn't there.

She'd known coming back to Barcelona would be difficult.

She just hadn't realised how lonely she would feel.

Diego lay in bed in the hospital's staff accommodation, staring up at the ceiling. He couldn't sleep. Couldn't lie still. Grace's last words to him were burning into his brain.

'Would it hurt you to show some compas-

*sion? To stop being a doctor and for once—
just once—show that you're a human being?'*

Frustration forced him to his feet, and he
pulled on a tee shirt and some trainers before
grabbing his phone and earbuds and heading out on a fast run.

The sun was beginning its slow journey
across the sky and already the temperature
was in the late twenties and promising mid
to late thirties. It was July. The middle of
summer. Already the streets of Barcelona
were filled with natives and tourists. Normally, they didn't bother him, but today he
took a thin alley between a couple of white-
washed buildings adorned with hanging
baskets and cracked blue mosaic tiles, that
took him away from the crowds perusing the
shops and storefronts towards the seafront,
where he could run on the promenade. The
sea air always made him feel good. There
was nothing quite like fresh air mixed with
the scent of the sea.

*'Would it hurt you to show some compas-
sion?'* The words echoed in his head.

Was that how she viewed him? A compas-
sionless monster? He thought he had shown
her how much he cared. He had been there
for her, holding her hand, mopping her tears

in the beginning. Had she forgotten those days? The days when he'd listened to her cry, when she'd doubled over sobbing, almost as if her grief were cutting her in two and she was trying to hold her broken pieces together?

He hadn't cried with her—had that been his mistake? He'd thought he was doing the right thing. That by staying strong he would allow her the room to fall apart. He'd understood her grief, her pain—he'd felt it too. But what would have been the point of both of them collapsing under the weight of their sorrow?

She'd needed him to be strong. She'd needed him to be factual. And, yes, maybe he had brought out the side of him that he used to cope with the families of sick babies in the neonatal unit. Maybe he was guilty of distancing himself. But it had been for *her*! Because he'd loved her and had wanted to be strong for her!

And now that strength was being used as a weapon to bash him with.

He wished he could tell her…let out all the pain that the loss of their three babies had caused him, too. The pain of the dreams that had been taken from him. His own childhood had been difficult—there'd been almost no time to be a child himself. So when he'd pictured himself as a father he'd told himself he would always be there for his children. Love them. Care for them. Have fun with them and show them the world. He'd dreamed of raising those children with Grace. Bilingually, if they could. They would have the brightest, most beautiful children together!

His chest began to burn as he ran harder and faster. The air was thick with heat, rather than oxygen, but he didn't care. He needed to run, needed to burn, needed to feel the pain of the muscles in his legs protesting, his lungs straining, his blood pumping. Needed to punish himself.

And that was when he saw her—Grace—sitting on a low wall, looking out to sea.

His steps slowed and he stopped a few metres short of her, panting heavily.

She must have sensed him, or something, because suddenly she turned, and when she saw him she quickly looked away and wiped at her eyes.

Had she been crying?

It was as if someone had punched him in the gut. Just the thought that she was in pain again broke him. So instead of challenging her and telling her that he wasn't a monster, that he *did* care, that he *did* feel compassion and that she had no right to accuse him of not having any, he pulled his earbuds out and walked over to her. Putting his own pain to one side yet again to put hers first.

Sitting down on the wall with his back to the sea, he waited for her to gather herself. Waited for her to be able to speak. He knew in that moment he would take the verbal bashing, whatever she needed, just as long as she stopped crying. That was something he couldn't bear to see. That was something he couldn't bear to be the cause of.

When he realised she had composed herself, he offered an olive branch. 'Carlita's baby was doing well when I left.'

He saw her nod in his peripheral vision.

'Good. I'm glad.'

He could hear her trying to be strong. To steady her voice.

'It's always a tricky thing when the mother has gestational diabetes. We'll keep an eye on him for a while. Make sure he doesn't get too jaundiced.'

'That's good.'

He thought about the next thing he wanted to say. Whether it would upset her or not. But he decided she might actually find comfort in it. 'They decided to call him Luca.'

She turned to look at him, then, her eyes searching his. Luca was the name they'd picked for their second baby, if he was a boy. It had always been a favourite name of Grace's. He hoped that she would view this piece of news as a good thing.

It seemed she did. Grace smiled. Then looked away to the sea again. He understood the peace it brought. He often came here to look out to sea. Mostly at sunrise.

The promenade was filled with people. Most of them headed to the beach, to fry themselves beneath the sun's strong rays.

'Couldn't sleep?' she asked him.

'No. You?'

'I haven't been back to the apartment yet.'

He liked this. Talking to her again without it being a battle. Okay, it wasn't as comfortable as he would have liked. He would have loved to have one of their usual conversations, where they told each other about their day, laughing over silly things, or sympathising over some of their harder cases. But this would do for now. This…ceasefire. Maybe they were able to talk like this because they weren't at home or at the hospital.

'You should try and get some rest,' he suggested.

'So should you.'

He smiled. She was right. And maybe he would be able to sleep now. Now that they'd spoken and now that her last words to him weren't accusatory ones.

She stood up from the wall, slung her bag over her shoulder. 'Aunt Felicity sends her love. She missed you. You always could wrap her around your little finger.'

'I missed seeing her, too.'

Grace folded her arms. 'We...er...we need to work out what we're going to tell people.'

He was confused. 'About what?'

'About us. And we'll need ground rules for when we see each other at work. No over-familiarity. No personal stuff. Let's just keep it professional, yes?'

He sucked in a breath, realising that her walls were going up again. He didn't like what she was saying, but what had he been expecting? He was the one who had moved out. He was the one who had stayed here whilst she went to Cornwall alone.

They had both agreed that their relationship was over. But he guessed knowing it and actually acting on it were two different things.

Grace was being sensible, that was all, and he would have to agree. Especially when it came to telling Isabella, his sister. He didn't want her rushing in and mothering him all over again, thinking that he needed it the way he had when they'd been children. Not now. Not when Isabella had other concerns on her mind. Concerns he'd not yet been able to tell Grace about.

How to tell Grace?

The guilt of knowing Isabella's big news when Grace didn't, and knowing it would hurt her when she did find out, made him agreeable. 'Sure. We can do that.'

'So, if anyone asks about us, what do I tell them? Just that we're over? That it didn't work out? Keep it simple and not embellish?'

He figured most of them would guess why. They all knew about the lost pregnancies. And who would want to probe into that mess? He didn't, so why would other people?

'Whatever you want.'

'I'm going to take you up to see your baby now.' Grace smiled as she went into her patient's room, pushing a wheelchair before her.

Amelia Lopez nodded and swung her legs out of bed, one hand holding her belly, where her caesarean incision was. Earlier that evening Amelia had been rushed into Theatre after suffering an early placenta praevia at just thirty-two weeks' gestation, and when her daughter had been born she'd been blue and floppy. Diego and his team had worked quickly to oxygenate Amelia's baby, and had whisked her away whilst the rest of the surgical team had continued to try to prevent Amelia haemorrhaging. It had been difficult, but they'd managed to staunch the blood before the decision to perform a hysterectomy had been made.

Since then Amelia had been recovering on the postnatal ward, hooked up to a blood transfusion, and her husband Joseph had gone home to shower and change, once he knew his wife and daughter were safe.

Grace set the brake on the wheelchair and then gently helped Amelia lower herself into it. She grabbed a blanket from the bed and draped it over Amelia's legs, because she felt a little cold still.

'How is she doing?' Amelia asked.

'As good as can be expected. When we get up there I'll get the doctor to come and talk to you. Explain what they've been doing and how they expect her to proceed.'

Amelia nodded.

'Have you thought of a name for her yet?'

'I'm not sure. I think I need to see her. I've not seen her face. I need to look at her and see what suits her.'

'Good idea.'

Grace began to push her out of the room and towards the lifts that would take them up another floor to the NICU. She felt great empathy with Amelia. How scared she must have been to feel that she was losing her child. And poor Joseph, her husband, who must have feared he was losing them both! But she was envious, too. Amelia and Joseph had been scared to death, terrified, fearful, and yet they'd still got their daughter. She was alive. Upstairs in a neonatal incubator. She had people fighting for her. Rooting for her. For these two, there was still the hope of a future with their child.

The lift doors pinged open and Grace wheeled Amelia inside, steeling herself for meeting Diego again.

Seeing him in Theatre earlier, those dark brown eyes of his smouldering above the surgical mask, she'd had to force herself to look away. To concentrate on what she was doing. Because when she looked at him, dressed in his scrubs, saving a baby, it did strange things to her insides.

He had skills she didn't understand. Knew how to do things she would never be able to get her head around. He could keep a steady hand when operating on a tiny baby, navigating his way around tiny organs, tiny hearts. He could go into a zone and somehow forget the tiny human on the table and just concentrate on fixing the problem, whatever it was. He could distance himself so that he could do his job, and it was something she both admired and feared. Because when she saw him doing that—doing the very best he could for his tiny patients and their families—it simply reminded her of why she'd fallen in love with him in the first place, and right now she didn't need to be reminded of why she loved him.

I need to remind myself of why I'm walking away.

She tried to steel herself as the lift doors pinged again and she wheeled Amelia out and headed for the NICU. She knew Diego would be there. Focused and sure and confident in his surroundings. This place was his castle and he ruled here. He was the king, and she had once loved to see him in his element here. Diego was intensely passionate about what he could do, and he had to be one of the best neonatal surgeons in the country. People came for miles, sometimes even from other countries, just to have him consult on their case. He was wanted. Desired. And not just by her.

As they got closer to the unit and she saw him there, his hands inside an incubator, listening to a baby's chest with a stethoscope, she gritted her teeth and wheeled Amelia in.

She felt his gaze upon her as soon as she came in. Like a warmth, an intensity washing over her. She glanced in his direction and met his eyes with her own. 'The Lopez baby?'

She watched as he looked at Amelia, then back up at Grace. 'She's over there in the far corner. Why don't you take Amelia over and I'll be there in just one moment to explain everything?'

'Thanks.' She tried to sound business-like. Professional. Not sad or wistful. But it was hard. Now that she was back, she knew she would have to start taking the steps to walk away, and at some point actually *tell*

Diego that she would be leaving. That would be much harder. Nerve-racking. She hadn't even told Renata yet. No one knew. Except her and Aunt Felicity.

She wheeled Amelia over to the incubator and set the brake once again. 'Here she is.'

Amelia peered through the side and tears welled up in her eyes. 'She's so tiny! Like a little bird!'

The baby was covered in wires and tubes. And although Grace knew what most of them were for, and what they did, she also knew that to Amelia they were strange and frightful things. Alien, almost. She was just about to start explaining what all of them were for, when she sensed Diego arriving beside them. She straightened up, nodded at him in acknowledgement.

'Mrs Lopez? I'm Dr Rivas, and I've been in charge of your daughter since you gave birth to her in Theatre.'

Grace stood back and let him take the lead. Allowing herself to listen and watch as he explained the condition of Amelia's daughter and what assistance she'd needed since being born. Apparently she had fluid in her lungs and needed a respirator, so that explained the tube down her throat. She also had wires monitoring her heart and her temperature. The little red light strapped to her big toe measured her oxygen saturations, and the tiny wrap around her arm measured blood pressure. She was holding steady. Doing as well as could be expected. They were monitoring her closely and she had a dedicated nurse, just for her.

Grace noted how his voice softened when he was talking to Amelia. How his eyes bloomed with a kindness and a sympathy that she loved—that she wished she'd seen and heard when they'd lost their own babies. It had been there at the beginning, but after that… He'd retreated from her.

Diego was talking to Amelia on her level, so that she would understand. He didn't use big, complicated medical terms; he kept it simple without being patronising. It was a difficult line to walk, but she could see that he was making Amelia feel confident that her baby was in good, strong and secure hands.

'Thank you, Dr Rivas. I appreciate everything you're doing for her. Can I touch her?'

He smiled broadly, the smile lighting up his eyes, and for Grace it was like a punch in the gut. 'Of course you can. There's a sink over there, where you can wash your hands first. Let me take you.'

Grace stepped back, clasping her hands behind her back so that she didn't touch Diego's accidentally on the handles of the wheelchair. Her heart was thudding hard in her chest and she was beginning to realise how hard it was going to be, keeping herself from him.

But I have to do it. There is no other way.

She looked at his broad back, at the shoulders she knew so well, and at the narrow waist around which she'd often draped an arm, resting her hand on his hip or caressing his bottom, the way she'd used to when they hadn't been able to keep their hands off one another. She missed that casual touching they had once done at work. Little ways in which they'd let the other know *I'm here... I love you.*

How long did it take for love to stop?

'I'll be doing night shifts exclusively for the next few weeks, so maybe it'll be good if—'

Diego bit his lip, hands on his hips, as they stood on the other side of the NICU while Amelia visited her daughter. 'Ah...'

She frowned, looking up at him, and he

couldn't help but be mesmerised, as he usually was, by her beauty.

'What do you mean by *ah*?'

He grimaced. 'You're going to suggest I do days, so that we can stay out of each other's way, aren't you?'

'No,' she answered, quietly but brusquely. 'I was thinking about Zara. If she's only wanting to deal with us, what if she needs one of us during the day? I thought it would make sense, if I'm doing nights, for you to do days.'

'Right. Only I'm already signed up to cover nights for the next month or so.'

'Oh.'

He couldn't read the expression on her face. Was it disappointment? Discomfort? Awkwardness? He'd hoped for something better than that. He wasn't sure why after that chat on the promenade, when she'd discussed with him different ways to tell people they'd broken up. He knew he'd been the one to move out, but that had been to give her space, to give her...

Who am I kidding? I did that for me! Because I couldn't bear to see her pain any more. Because I couldn't bear to feel so helpless.

But to actually start telling people they were over…? That was a different kettle of fish. It was like telling people you were expecting a baby. The more people you told, the more real it became.

He didn't want to think that he and Grace were over. He'd hoped that somehow, somewhere, there was still a little love left to salvage.

But how can there be? All I do is cause her pain by giving her babies she can't keep, and then I have to watch the fallout! I'm bad for her. I always have been. Dragging her away from the home she knew to this place. Putting her through what I have and somehow expecting her to still love me. Loco.

'I'll try to stay out of your way—except for when we're with Zara, of course. If that will make it better for you.' It pained him to offer this, but what else could he do? He had to let go of the woman he loved. Give her the chance to find happiness elsewhere. Even if it killed him to see her with someone else.

He instantly felt sick at the thought.

She nodded, not meeting his gaze. 'Fine.'

And then she went back over to Amelia, a bright smile pasted on her face, and it physically pained him to watch her walk away.

He knew it was something he would have to get used to. But at least she was still here. At least he could see her for now.

It wasn't as if she was about to leave Spain and return home, never to be seen again.

At the end of her shift Grace didn't feel tired at all, so she headed for the staff swimming pool.

St Aelina's was a modern hospital, designed by a very sought-after architect who had blended the building itself into the local area, artfully hiding the solar panels among the rooftops and cultivating St Aelina's Park behind it, which was filled with sculptures and water features created by local artists.

The hospital itself had obviously been designed to cater for its patients with the best technology and equipment, but it also prided itself on looking after its staff's physical and mental wellbeing. Apart from the pool, with its low dive board, there was a sauna, a steam room, a gymnasium, a juice bar, and also a quiet library, a sensory room and a staff counsellor on site.

Although Grace loved the peacefulness and quiet of the library, today she felt the need to be in the water. Hopefully no one else would be there, and she would be able to swim a few lengths and then relax by just floating on her back for a while and closing her eyes.

She got her wish. No one was there at this time of the morning, and as the early sun beamed through the floor-to-ceiling windows, she dived in, swimming for a few metres underwater, before surfacing and performing a powerful front crawl from one end of the twenty-five-metre pool to the other.

For a moment the exercise did what it was meant to do. She forgot everything. Diego. Their both being on nights for the foreseeable future. And the fact that at some point she would have to tell him she was leaving.

She would have to tell Renata, her boss, too. She didn't want to let her down, but what else could she do? She couldn't stay and see Diego every day.

The water soothed her. She'd grown acclimatised to the chemical tang of chlorine in the air and she powered through the water as if all that mattered was getting from one end to the other. As her lungs began to burn and her muscles protested she slowed, flipped onto her back, and let her residual energy float her gently into the heart of the pool.

She closed her eyes and gently began to paddle her arms to stay afloat. She heard the door at the poolside open, but ignored it. All that mattered was the floating. The feeling of being in warm water and all her cares floating away...

She heard a splash. Someone diving into the water. She heard them swimming, but paid no more attention.

Just float. That's all you have to do...

When she finally began to feel hungry, and knew she ought to get dressed, go home and try to get some rest, she straightened and swam breaststroke to the edge of the pool, hauling herself onto the side and wrapping her towel around her. When she turned, she stopped, her breath suddenly caught in her throat.

It was Diego. He was the person who had been swimming. He was the person even now up on the dive board, adjusting his footing preparing to dive in.

Her gaze hungrily raked over his body. This was an unexpected gift. The body she knew intimately. And the sudden, gut-wrenching yearning she felt for him almost left her breathless.

But she knew she couldn't stay and stare

at him when he suddenly locked eyes with her. She saw a range of emotions cross his face, but the one that was strongest was regret. He looked down at the water, took a breath, and dived in.

She knew she couldn't dive back into the water and swim into his arms, the way she once might have done. Instead, sadly, she turned away and headed back to the changing room, unaware that he watched her go.

CHAPTER FOUR

'How ARE THINGS going for you back there? Have you seen Diego?' asked Aunt Felicity over the phone.

Grace had been honest with her aunt when she'd visited. Told her everything that she and Diego had been through. And, bless her, her aunt had sat and listened and had not been judgmental about either of them.

'We've spoken.'

'How did he take the news that you're coming home?'

Grace shifted in her seat. 'I haven't told him yet.'

'What? Grace, you have to tell him. He deserves to know. Unless…'

As her aunt trailed off, Grace sipped at her coffee. 'Unless what?'

'Unless you're having second thoughts. I'd understand if so. You've made a life over there. A commitment. It will be hard for you to leave that—especially if you still have feelings for him.'

Grace shook her head. 'There are no second thoughts.'

'But there *are* feelings?'

Grace paused to think. Of course there were. You didn't marry someone and move to a whole other country and try to have three babies with him and not have feelings. But... 'Not like that.'

'Oh, Grace, honey... You know you can be honest with me.'

'I am! He left me feeling alone, remember? He could barely look at me. Once he realised I was faulty goods, he couldn't get away fast enough.'

'People deal with grief in different ways.'

'So, I'm just supposed to accept abandonment and carry on like nothing ever happened?'

'No, I'm not saying that. I'm saying that maybe you need to tell him how you feel.'

'I did. And he moved out. Remember?' Grace shook her head. 'You always did have a soft spot for Diego, like he could do no wrong.'

'That's not fair, honey, and you know that.

I love you, and I have raised you to be a strong woman, I think. It's just that sometimes you…'

'What?'

'Sometimes you don't always give people a chance to explain.'

'I begged him to tell me what he was feeling. I begged him to show me some kind of emotion, and he walked away.'

'Maybe he found it difficult. Maybe he was trying so hard to be strong for you that he forgot he also needed to share his feelings.'

'No. No, Diego isn't like that.' She felt sure of it. *Didn't she?* This conversation wasn't going the way she'd expected it to. 'Anyway, I haven't told anyone I'm leaving yet. We're short-staffed, and I've offered to cover nights for the next few weeks.'

There was a sigh at the other end. 'You need to tell Renata if you're planning to leave.'

'I will. When I'm ready.'

'Maybe Diego will talk to you when *he's* ready, too.'

Everywhere he looked, it seemed Grace was there. At the hospital, in the pool, on the wards, in the hospital cafeteria, on the promenade…and now the operating room. His wife stood opposite him, waiting to collect the baby after he'd finished its surgery in utero.

The baby was at thirty-eight weeks and had been developing a small, non-cancerous growth on its neck over the last couple of weeks that, on ultrasound, looked like a cyst. He'd decided to perform a caesarean section and operate on the baby before cutting the cord, so that the cord could continue to supply blood and oxygen until the cyst was excised, the wound stitched. Then he would complete the caesarean and deliver the baby.

Normally in Theatre he felt as if he could do anything. This was where he excelled— this was where he thrived. But since moving out of his home with Grace even the happiness he got from being in Theatre was dampened.

He should be feeling happy. The cyst excision had gone perfectly. And yet when he'd looked up to meet Grace's eyes and smile at his success she hadn't been looking at him. Instead she'd just stood there, eyes cast downwards, with a sterile cloth draped over her hands, waiting to receive the baby.

It was like being stabbed in the heart. This had been one of their things. Operating together and on a successful outcome meeting each other's eyes and smiling.

He'd felt her dismissal at the pool, too. Up on that diving board, ready to slice through the water, he had known she was looking at him and he'd met her gaze. But he'd realised all too quickly that they could never be what they'd been before. He'd seen it in her eyes. She blamed him for everything. For leaving her. For treating her badly, as she saw it, and being the one who'd caused her all that pain in the first place.

He'd not been able to stay on that board a moment longer under her accusatory glare, so he'd dived into the water. And when he'd surfaced she'd been leaving, and he'd had to stop swimming, feeling all the air gone from his body as he ached for her so badly it had physically pained him. So much so that he'd pulled himself from the water and sat on the poolside, struggling to control his breathing.

It was like losing a piece of himself. As if someone had chopped off a limb. No, not that. As if someone had dug out his heart and left a gaping, bloody hole in his chest.

He missed her so much. Missed her smile

when she looked at him. Missed the sound of her laughter. The feel of her at his side.

The better part of him was gone and it was all his fault.

Diego clamped the cord and passed her the baby. She turned away to take it to the Resuscitaire, and he returned to finish off the section.

Had she told anyone yet? That they were over? He'd told Isabella that they were having problems, but he'd kept it vague and hadn't even mentioned that the marriage was probably over. He'd made it sound as if they'd had a bit of a tiff and it would all blow over.

Perhaps he needed to face facts. Instead of looking at his wife with regret and longing, he should just accept the truth. Did he really want to be a man who walked around the hospital pining for his wife?

They'd been through too much.

It was too late for them.

What they'd had was lost.

After the surgery Grace was having a well-earned rest. It was just after two o'clock in the morning and all was quiet on the wards. Today she was looking after the postnatal ward, and most of the mothers and their babies were asleep. All the lights were down except for the ones at the midwives' desk, and so she sat there, holding one of the babies, appreciating the quiet and the solitude.

To her there was something special about the night shift. It was weird, because when she'd first started doing shift work she'd hated nights. Hated the disruption it caused in her life, playing around with her sleep schedule. But now that she was an experienced midwife she actually preferred them. The phones didn't ring constantly, upper management weren't always walking around, and she didn't have to cope with streams of visitors coming and going.

Night shifts were quiet. Just the sound of soft shoes on tiles, the occasional cry of a baby, the gentle murmuring of mother's voices as they tried to soothe or feed their newborns. And if she needed to help anyone—help a mother breastfeed, show her how to latch the baby on so that she didn't get pain—then there was an intimacy to doing that in the middle of the night. Mothers who had just given birth were tired and happy and grateful, and Grace was always ready to go and make an exhausted mother a hot chocolate, or some toast, or even take a baby for a little while and give it a cuddle, just so its mum could get some sleep.

And that was what she was doing now.

In her arms she held baby Arlo. His mum Emilia had been in labour all day yesterday and she'd only given birth a few hours ago. The poor woman was exhausted, but once she'd fed her son he hadn't seemed to want to settle in his cot. Grace had offered to take him for a while, so that Emilia could sleep.

Gazing down at the baby now, she couldn't help but smile and stroke his fat cheek, and marvel at the wonder that was a newborn child.

'That suits you.'

Diego.

She looked up. How had she not heard him approach? Her cheeks flushed, but she looked down at Arlo and continued to rock him. She was not sure what she could say to this man she was trying her hardest not to be around.

'I can't do this, Grace.'

She heard the upset in his voice and it pulled at her. Pulled at her heartstrings. She heard real angst there, real emotion—and, damn it, wasn't that what she'd begged him to show her? She couldn't ignore it now.

'Can't do what?'

Arlo grizzled slightly at the sound of her voice, but then settled down again.

Diego stared down at her from the other side of the desk. 'I can't do my job with you ignoring me. With you not even able to look at me. We used to be close...we used to be...' He stopped and bit his lip before changing tack. 'I need to be able to talk to you. We need to be civil.'

'You're talking about what happened in Theatre?'

He nodded.

She thought about his words. About how hard it had been in Theatre for her to ignore him. Not to look at him in his scrubs, not to remind herself that this gorgeous, amazing man was no longer hers, not to fall in love again with his skills and abilities and talent.

Talent and intelligence. Two things that Grace found incredibly attractive and sexy. And Diego had both of those and much more. Today this man in front of her had performed surgery on a baby in utero! If people knew how much study that took—how much training, how many hours of education and learning had to go into something like that—they'd be amazed. And yet Diego had done so easily and without breaking a sweat. She might not have watched his face, but she had watched his hands. His fingers. How skilfully and surely they had manipulated the instruments. No shaking. No nerves. Just precision. Skill. Talent. The irrefutable knowledge that what he was doing was right. It had been powerful and dizzying stuff.

'This isn't easy for me either, Diego.'

'You think it is for me?'

She met his gaze, shocked, hearing again a little surge of frustration in his voice. She'd thought it *was* easy for him. He was the one who had walked away!

'We work together, Grace. And we've got to work together on Zara. If that girl is going to trust us, then we've at least got to show that we're partners. In work, if nothing else.'

He was right. She knew it.

'You ignoring me, not looking at me, refusing to speak to me, even to acknowledge that I'm in the same room as you...' He stared at her as if he couldn't quite believe she had acted in such a way. 'It's disrespectful. But more than that it's hurtful.'

So he *was* capable of feeling hurt? Grace

gazed at her husband, then looked down at the baby in her arms. If only she'd been able to have one of her own then they wouldn't be in this mess. Her husband wouldn't be on the other side of a desk, telling her that she was hurting him. She wouldn't have failed him. That was why he was angry now. She had failed him and she was failing him again.

He had married her, thinking that she would give him the huge family that he had dreamed of. And she'd failed him. Over and over again.

Her aunt's voice came back to her *'Maybe Diego will talk to you when he's ready.'*

Maybe he was ready now?

'You're right. I apologise. From now on I will be perfectly civil.'

He stared at her, almost as if he were checking to make sure that she wasn't playing with him. But she stared back at him, determined and sincere.

'All right. Thank you.'

She saw his gaze drop to the baby in her arms again and his face filled with sorrow.

'It really does suit you, you know.'

Then he was gone, disappearing from the light and into the shadows of the corridor.

* * *

Diego knocked on Zara's door and went in when he heard her say that he could. 'Hi. Just thought I'd see how you are. You've had a lot of information to take in over the last few days.'

She must have just woken up. It was early. Seven a.m. Her hair was all mussed, her face swollen with sleep.

'I'm okay. It's weird sleeping inside.' She glanced at the window. The sun was beginning to stream in through the blinds.

'But better than sleeping on the ground?' He grabbed her notes from the end of the bed and sat on the chair beside her. 'Any more pains?' He flicked through her notes, noting that she seemed stable. Her blood pressure was good and the traces she'd had showed that her baby was doing well.

'No. I think the antibiotics are working.'

'That's good. I thought I'd let you know that Grace and I will be working nights, if you need us. But I can pop in during the day, too. I often work overtime or stay late. Just ask one of the midwives to page me.'

She looked at him curiously. 'When do you sleep?'

He smiled. 'Not often these days. And

mostly in on-call rooms. It just seems easier, if there's an emergency I need to rush to.'

She tucked a strand of hair behind her ears. 'Is my baby going to be okay? He's got a lot wrong with him.'

'I know it's scary to have to sit and listen to doctors using all these medical terms, when your expectation is that your baby will be healthy and like everybody else's, but it's a good thing, Zara. We know what he needs, so that when he's born there's no complications. No panic. We know what we're doing and we'll look after him.'

She bit her lip and he saw her glance at the door. Was this girl a flight risk?

'I don't want you to run,' he said. 'Think about what will happen if you do. You'll go back into the world—an *uncaring* world that will see you back on the street. And if you give birth out there, to a baby that needs medical intervention to survive, you could lose him. But here...with us...' He implored her with his eyes. 'We can give him the very best start, with your help.'

She nodded. 'Okay. Thank you.'

Diego stood and smiled down at her. 'I'll leave you be. No doubt breakfast will be here soon. I just wanted to pop in and let you know that if you don't see us around too much during the day it doesn't mean we've forgotten you.'

He needed the save on this one. He didn't want her running away with fear. They had every chance to help this baby and, having lost three of his own, every save gave him back hope. Every save made him extremely happy indeed. Made him feel useful.

'And I can page you whenever I need to?'

He nodded. 'Whenever you need to you can have them call me. Night *or* day.'

He hoped that now he'd talked to Grace, and she'd promised to be civil, working together on Zara from now on would be a lot more pleasant.

He liked spending time with her, and had missed her like crazy when she was gone. Part of him had feared she would never return, and if that had happened he didn't know what he would have done. Gone after her? Begged her to come back?

But she had come back, and when he'd seen her in that corridor the first time he had felt such relief! Such joy. Along with the realisation that they still had so much to say to one another. So much to sort out. He wasn't ready to lose her. All of this didn't seem real, and he was actually thankful that he had Zara as a patient, to work on with Grace. It would give them plenty of opportunity to talk—professionally and, he hoped, privately.

Persuading Zara to stay was one thing.

Persuading Grace might be another thing entirely.

And what would I be asking her to stay for?

Grace was being paged to the ER. As senior midwife during the night shift the onus was on her, but she was happy enough to leave the maternity floor in the capable hands of her colleagues. They weren't too busy that night. Zara was fast asleep, and the two labouring mums they had in were still at their early stages—only three to four centimetres dilated and contracting irregularly.

Carlos, a nurse in the ER, had asked for her after a woman had been brought in with a pelvic bleed. She was eighteen weeks pregnant.

Hearing the symptoms made her heart almost stop. Instantly she knew what this woman must be feeling. What she must be fearing was happening. Was she losing her baby?

Grace put down the phone and stared at it for a moment. She wondered if she was strong enough for this. Would she be able to get through it without becoming emotional herself? Eighteen weeks was too soon to deliver. The baby would not survive. This bleed the patient was experiencing might be nothing, but what if it was something terrible? What if she had to sit with this woman whilst she lost her baby?

Could I handle that?

She picked up the phone again, dialled the number that would ring the doctors' line in Neonatal.

'Dr Rivas, neonatal surgeon.'

'It's me.'

'Grace? What's wrong?'

She could hear the concern in his voice, and it was almost like the time when she'd had to ring him after she'd begun to miscarry their second baby.

She'd been at home, folding laundry, getting ready to put the clothes away, when she'd experienced sharp, stabbing pains in her womb that had made her double over.

She'd sat down on the edge of their bed and taken a few deep breaths, thinking it was over, that it hadn't been anything serious. Then the pains had come back. Fiercer. Stronger. So much so she'd cried out and scrambled for her mobile phone on the bedside cabinet.

She'd somehow made it to the bathroom, pulled down her clothes and seen the first signs of blood. She'd tried to dial his number, her trembling fingers misdialling at first, and by the time she had rung the blood had been flowing.

'Hey?'

'Diego...'

'Grace? What's wrong?'

He'd heard it. In her voice. The upset, the terror. The tears. It all came back to her now.

She swallowed hard. 'I need you to meet me in the ER.'

'Okay. Why?'

'I've been paged for a woman with a pelvic bleed. She's eighteen weeks.' She knew she didn't have to say any more. Knew that he would understand her trepidation about going down there and facing this alone.

'I'll be right down.'

She nodded and put down the phone, hearing her pulse thrumming in her ears, feeling light-headed, weak. If Diego was there, perhaps he would be able to speak and offer comfort when she couldn't? This was going to be hard. A real test for her. She'd not been called down for a bleed as early as this since her own losses. Now she would be on the other side, and she had no idea how helpful she'd be.

Ana, busy scribbling notes into a patient record, asked her if she was okay? 'Do you want me to go instead?'

'No. I should do it. I have to do it sometime.'

Ana nodded. 'Okay. But I'm here if you want me to take over at any point.'

She appreciated that. 'I won't be long.'

Grace headed down to the ER, thanking whatever gods might be listening for the lift that took ages to arrive, for the slow ride down, giving her the time to steel herself, to prepare, to try to be strong.

The patient was going to need her strength. Her comfort. Her reassurances. Her patient was going to need a professional—not a bumbling mess.

As she got down to the ER she saw that Diego was already there, chatting to a male nurse. The one who'd called her? And that he'd seen her arrive.

He came straight over to her. She was instantly taken by the way he looked. The determined stride, his face sincere, yet with that professional distance. Clearly he was more ready for this patient than she was.

'Grace, thanks for calling me.'

She shrugged, so nervous it was almost as if her teeth were about to start chattering. 'I just thought that together we'd be able to—'

He shook his head. 'No. I think I should see her alone.'

'But I was the one paged. I know how she's feeling!'

'I know. I can see it in your eyes. And you cannot go in there looking and feeling the way you do.'

'Diego, I—'

He placed his hand on her shoulder and his touch did remarkable things. Her voice stopped working, her body came alive and her heart, which had already been thrumming hard, seemed suddenly able to jump out of her body and go hopping along down the corridor with every beat.

'Let me take this. Let me perform a scan.

Then, and only then, I will decide whether you should be involved.'

She knew what he was doing. He was trying to protect her. She got that. She really did! But all she heard was Diego telling her what to do and deciding what was best for her. When really those decisions were her own to make.

'*I* was paged. *I* was called. This is my patient. I called you to *assist*. We go in together.' She didn't mean to sound so harsh with him, but she couldn't help it. He'd actually infuriated her.

He stared hard into her eyes, looking exasperated, and then nodded with reluctance. 'Okay.'

He stepped back and let her lead the way.

Grace dropped her shoulders, lifted her chin, took a deep breath and asked the nurse which cubicle their patient was in.

'Cubicle five. She was here earlier today.'

'Thank you.'

She led the way, her stomach in turmoil, her mouth dry. She hoped beyond hope that this was just a benign bleed. That this was not going to be a loss. She wasn't sure if she could watch the same thing she had experienced happen to another woman. She knew it was part of the job, and that this kind of thing happened, but it had more impact when you'd been through it yourself.

Grace had lain in an ER bed. She'd been the patient. She'd been the one who had had a midwife called down to her. It had been Renata. Her boss. And although she'd always viewed Renata as a woman who could be firm, yet fair, on that occasion, with Grace crying in the bed, Renata had been wonderfully kind. Sympathetic. Honest. And yet also the kind of professional that Grace had needed. She might have been among her colleagues and her friends, but that day they had been her medical team, more than anything else. They had found the distance they'd needed to treat her and care for her.

Grace pulled open the curtain and saw a woman curled up on the bed. She looked to be in her thirties, wearing a set of pyjamas. Her heart ached for her. This woman must have gone to bed thinking it was just another day. That everything was normal. Before her world came crashing down.

'Hi. My name's Grace and I'm a midwife, and this is Diego Rivas, a doctor.' She didn't want to say neonatal surgeon. Didn't want this woman instantly thinking of surgery and blood and emergencies. Not yet. Not whilst there was still hope. 'What's your name?'

'Mia. Mia Fernandez'

'Tell us what's happening, Mia,' she said gently.

'There was a car accident. This afternoon. Nothing huge. Just someone rear-ended me whilst I was stationary, waiting for some kids to cross the road. No damage to the cars. Nothing. I just had a little backache. A small pain in my neck. I came to the ER this afternoon and got checked out. Everything was fine.'

'Okay.' Grace nodded. Smiled. Encouraging her. Not rushing her. She picked up the patient notes at the end of the bed, opened them, began reading today's earlier admittance information. Mia was right. Everything had checked out. Baby and mum had seemed fine.

'I went home. Had a bath. Then I went to bed and fell asleep. But I woke around midnight with pains, and then I noticed the bleeding and I...' Mia began crying again. 'Please... I don't want to lose my baby!'

Grace's blood ran cold. They were the

same words that she had cried out. She remembered pleading with Renata. With the ER doctor who had been attending her at the time. The memories it brought back were sharp and painful. Like a knife cutting open an old wound.

Suddenly she couldn't speak, and she looked imploringly to Diego.

He stepped forward. 'We're going to do an ultrasound, Mia, is that okay? And we may have to examine you…make sure you're not dilating.'

Mia nodded quickly, her long hair obscuring her face as she sobbed.

Grace was grateful that Diego had stepped in when she couldn't speak. She offered to fetch the ultrasound machine. It would give her time to gather herself. Catch her breath. Get control of all the memories that were flooding in.

As she began to wheel the machine back towards cubicle five Diego met her, his face full of concern. 'Maybe you should sit this out?'

'I'm fine.'

'The hell you are. Look at you—your hands are shaking.'

She stopped pushing the ultrasound and

folded her arms, hating it that he had seen that. 'I need to see this through.'

'Why?'

'Because I'm a professional and this is my job.'

'You lost three babies, Grace. No one would blame you if you sat this out.'

She looked up at him. Frowned. 'You mean *we* lost three babies. And if you can be in there, then so can I.'

She began to push the machine again, furious that he had implied that she somehow couldn't do her job because of her loss. Only it hadn't just been *her* loss, but theirs. Or had he already moved on? If he had, she envied him that ability. She had no idea how he could even be in that cubicle with Mia and not feel *something*.

But that had been the problem all along, hadn't it?

'I'm just going to scan you, Mia, okay? You'll feel the cold gel and then I'll use this wand to take a look inside. It shouldn't hurt, but if it does you tell me, okay?'

Mia nodded, lying back and lifting up her pyjama top.

Grace eyed her small bump. 'Is this your first?'

Mia nodded again.

'And do you have someone we can call?'

She shook her head. 'No. I have no family and the father is away. He works on an oil rig.'

Grace hoped her hand was no longer trembling now that she was using the ultrasound wand, and as she moved it over Mia's abdomen she began to see the baby. It was moving. Its heart was beating. She smiled, feeling relief flood through her.

'Look.'

Mia peered at the screen, frowning, then a hesitant smile crept onto her face. 'It's okay?'

'It is. And the placenta looks fine, too.' She measured the heart rate. It was perfect. Exactly as they'd expect. The bleeding wasn't happening because the placenta was separating. At least not from what she could see. 'We'll need to run some more tests, and we'll want to keep you in for rest and observation—is that okay?'

Mia beamed, nodding. 'Absolutely. Do what you have to. Whatever keeps my baby safe.'

Grace removed the probe. 'I'll order those

tests.' She wheeled the machine away, returning it to his place, and let out a heavy sigh. So far it was looking good for Mia's baby. She was glad. And envious. She couldn't help it.

'Baby's okay—that's good.' Diego was at her side.

She glanced at him, straightening the cable and the plug. 'It is.'

'She'll need to stay in for a while. Observation.'

Grace nodded. 'I've told her that already. And that we'll probably run some tests to check where the bleeding is coming from.'

'It might just be her cervix. Sometimes it gets—'

'I *do* know, Diego. I'm a qualified midwife, remember?'

He looked about them. One or two people had looked their way when she'd raised her voice.

She blushed, annoyed that she'd drawn attention to them. 'Sorry. I didn't mean to…' She sighed. 'I guess this has just got to me a little bit.'

He nodded. 'I understand.'

'*Do* you, Diego?' She stared at him, curious. Did he truly understand just how this had affected her?

He met her gaze. 'I always have.'

CHAPTER FIVE

THE NEXT FEW night shifts passed in a blur. Grace was present for her patients, helping them welcome their babies into the world, celebrating with them, rejoicing, admiring their newborns and genuinely telling each of them how precious and how beautiful they were. But each morning when she got home again, back to her empty flat, she felt as if she'd been working on automatic.

Something was missing. Whether it was from the job, or just something at St Aelina's, or whether it was to do with Diego she wasn't sure. She just knew she didn't feel as fulfilled as she normally did after a shift.

When Diego had told her that he'd always understood how she felt after seeing Mia Fernandez, who was now safely at home, still pregnant—it had been a bleed from a lesion on her cervix—she'd found herself looking for him, wondering, wanting to ask more, but the last few nights she'd hardly seen him.

'I've heard one of the paramedics is seeing a nurse in the ER,' said Gabbi, as she and Mira and Grace had sat together, sharing a rare moment and enjoying a cup of coffee together.

Grace shrugged. 'It's not surprising.'

'Don't you know?'

'Know what?'

'I'm talking about Carlos.'

Carlos. The nurse she'd spoken to when she went down to see Mia. 'Oh. Well, good for him. He's a good-looking guy.'

'He's going out with your sister-in-law! Hasn't Diego said?' Mira asked in surprise.

Isabella? 'No, he…er…'

'Is everything okay between you two?'

Grace felt her cheeks colour, having hoped to avoid this conversation entirely. 'Things have been…difficult lately.'

Mira and Gabbi exchanged glances. 'Sorry, we didn't mean to interfere. You don't have to say if you don't want to.'

'No, it's fine. It's just…it's been difficult since the miscarriages, you know?'

'We get it.' They shared another look, and

Mira mouthed something to Gabbi. Then Gabbi was shaking her head as if to say, *No, not right now.*

'What is it?' asked Grace.

Gabbi looked at her wide-eyed. Innocent. 'Nothing.'

'Tell me, Gabs.'

Gabbi looked at Mira once more, then turned to face Grace. 'It's just that there's rumours that…'

'What?'

'That Isabella's pregnant.'

Grace felt as if she'd been punched in the gut. Her mind whirled with thoughts and emotions, none of them pleasant, or feelings that made her feel particularly proud. Jealousy was the main one.

But then she focused on her friend's words. 'Rumours. Not fact?'

Gabbi and Mira nodded. 'Just hearsay.'

Grace sipped her coffee. It had to be hearsay. Diego would have told her if that was the truth, surely? He had seemed distracted lately. They were getting used to working together in a new way now, but it was difficult being thrown together to work on a case when they couldn't be the people they used to be—husband and wife.

He would have told me.

Wouldn't he? Or did he feel that he couldn't? That by telling her he would somehow be rubbing salt into the wounds of their still raw losses?

No. He would have said. This had to be a rumour. It couldn't be anything else. If Isabella was pregnant, then... A wave of sadness washed over her and she suddenly felt as if she could cry. Was that why Isabella hadn't stayed to talk to her the night she'd brought in Zara? Was that why Isabella had hardly looked her in the eye? Was that why Diego looked at her as if he was frightened of how she might react after her outburst before she went to Cornwall?

'Excuse me.' Grace took her mug to the privacy of the small kitchenette, tipping the rest of her suddenly bitter drink into the sink and taking a deep breath before washing cold water over her face.

Rumours in hospitals spread like wildfire.

They weren't always true.

She had to believe that if this one was, then Diego would have had the good grace and the respect to inform her.

She would ask him to tell her the truth the next time she saw him.

* * *

'I thought I'd let you know that you are no longer showing any signs of infection.' Diego smiled at Zara as he scribbled a note into her medical file.

'So I'm healthy?'

'At the moment.'

'Are you going to put me back on the streets?'

He met her gaze, shocked that she'd ask. 'No, of course not. Why would you even think that?'

Zara shrugged. 'I guess I'm just not used to people looking out for me. They normally can't wait to get rid of me.'

He put her notes back in the slot at the end of her bed and then sat down on the chair beside her. 'We're not going to do that. You're vulnerable. Young. Your baby is going to need attention when he's born and we're going to keep you here until you're both fit and well. Okay?'

'And after that?'

He didn't know. Though he'd like to try and help her out. Maybe find her some accommodation for her and her son.

'And what if he doesn't make it? He's safe right now, inside me. I can look after him.

But when he's born he's going to have all those problems and…' Zara began to cry.

Diego passed her a box of tissues and waited. 'I know you're scared. It's normal to feel that way. But he can't stay inside you for ever, and when he's born you'll have a crack team of specialists to support both of you.'

'You'll perform his surgery?'

He nodded. 'I will.'

'And you'll be honest with me? I don't want you to lie to me. I know I'm only eighteen, but I am going to be his mother and so I'll deserve to know the truth!'

'I will be honest with you.'

'You promise?'

He nodded again. 'I promise. Now, how about we get you in a wheelchair and I take you for a bit of fresh air in the park?'

It was the middle of the day and Diego felt the need for some sunshine. He loved nights, he really did, but he just needed to bask in the warm rays of the sunshine on occasion.

Zara smiled. 'Deal.'

Grace hadn't slept very well, and she had a headache because of it as she went in for her next night shift. She kept alert, looking for Diego, needing to talk to him about Isabella. He'd know for sure if his sister was pregnant or not, and although Grace didn't want to let hospital gossip fuel her fears and worries, this one struck quite close to home.

She knew she could call Isabella and ask her herself, but she didn't know how she would react if Isabella confirmed the news. False cheer? Pretending to be thrilled for her whilst being swamped with jealousy? And if Isabella just laughed and told her it was gossip it would make Grace look as if she was someone who avidly listened to the hospital grapevine. Was nosy.

No. It was Diego she needed to talk to.

She placed her bag and jacket in her locker and headed onto the ward for the hand-over.

Renata stood at the front of the small room and gave them the information. Three labouring mothers currently on the labour ward. A first-time mother at forty-one weeks, who'd come in that morning to be induced and was currently at five centimetres, a second-time mother who was labouring with a twin pregnancy, currently at four centimetres, and a mother who was labouring with her first, at seven centimetres dilated.

'Grace? I'd like you to take her, if you

don't mind? She's in room six. Sofia Grayson. She's only thirty-six weeks, so I've notified Neonatal and they're sending down your husband.'

Grace nodded. 'Okay.'

So she would get to see Diego tonight. Speak to him quietly about this ridiculous rumour that was going around. Set things straight. Because he wouldn't have kept something like that from her, would he?

But have I really given him the opportunity to tell me?

She pushed that thought to one side. She was not going to take the blame for that. Diego had had plenty of opportunity to tell her anything. On the promenade that morning a few days ago. Down in the ER when they'd met over Mia's case. They'd chatted privately then. He would have said, surely?

No. He wouldn't have said, because it's not true!

That was why Diego hadn't said anything.

Grace put her notes into her pocket and headed down to room six. She said hello to Sofia and her English husband, Henry, then caught up on the case from the day-shift midwife, who updated her. Sofia was contracting well and regularly and making good progress.

Henry stood to one side of his wife's bed, holding her hand.

'So, how did you two meet?' Grace asked.

She liked to ask a couple of questions to her labouring mothers and parents-to-be. It helped establish a bond of trust and allowed each of them to get to know one another a little better. Sometimes it relaxed the mum-to-be to talk about something other than the human about to exit her body in a painful way.

Henry smiled at his wife. 'She was an air hostess on my flight from London to Barcelona. She charmed me with her offers of coffee and snacks.'

Sofia smiled too. 'The way to a man's heart is through his stomach.' Then she sucked on her gas and air as another contraction came. She was coping quite well with them and hadn't had any other form of pain relief.

'What do you do, Henry?'

'I'm a chef.'

'Interesting! And you live here in Barcelona?'

He nodded. 'To be with this woman, I'd

live anywhere.' Henry smiled at her. 'You're English. How come you work here?'

'Similar thing. My husband is Spanish. I came out here to live.'

'Oh? And what does he do?'

At that moment there was a knock on the door.

Grace smiled, feeling her heart suddenly pound. 'If this is who I think it is, then I'll let him tell you himself. Come in!'

The door opened and there he was. Looking fresh and perfect and just as handsome as he always did. Those dark chocolate eyes of his were intense and yet dreamy. He was in his scrubs already, soft curls of hair at the nape of his neck, his four o'clock shadow stumbling his jaw. His dark olive skin was perfect, his biceps strong and delicious.

Just the sight of him standing there, with his stethoscope casually draped around his neck, and the way his gaze instantly went to her before turning to the parents-to-be in the room, and the way he was giving them the benefit of that charming, attractive, *you-can-trust-me-I'm-a-professional* smile... Would she ever stop physically reacting to the sight of him?

'I'm Dr Rivas and I'm a neonatal surgeon.

I thought I'd come down to introduce myself. Nothing to worry about. I'm just here because you're with us a few weeks earlier than expected.'

Sofia and Henry said hello.

Then Diego came towards Grace.

He smiled at her—a soft smile, a *hello* smile—and picked up Sofia's trace to take a look at how she and the baby were doing.

Grace knew he'd find nothing wrong with it. Baby Grayson was doing well. Tolerating the contractions and without decels. She gazed up at Diego, wishing she could ask him right now about Isabella, but now was not the time. Instead, she took a moment to study his profile, to take in those lips she knew so well, the prominent cheekbones, the roman nose that had been broken when he was a teenager, the thick dark lashes around those eyes of his…

'This all looks good. How are you feeling, Sofia?'

Sofia nodded, completely under Diego's spell. 'I'm feeling good.'

'Excellent.' Diego beamed. 'That's what we like to hear.'

Grace wished she could ask him to step outside, so she could ask about Isabella, but she knew that if she did Sofia and Henry might think the conversation was about them and that something was wrong. She didn't want her patients to think she was keeping secrets from them. This job was all about patients being able to put their trust in the professionals.

'How are you?' she whispered to her husband.

He looked at her, as if surprised that she'd asked.

'I'm good,' he said in a low voice. 'You?'

'Good.' She nodded, itching to ask. But this was not the place. 'I'd like to speak to you when you have a moment free.'

Now he turned the full force of his gaze upon her. 'Is something wrong?'

'No. Just something I need to ask you.'

Diego nodded. 'Okay. When I get a free moment I'll page you.'

'Sounds good.'

He *smelled* good. She could smell that bodywash that he liked to use in the shower. It was doing dizzying things to her brain. Scent could be such a powerful thing when it came to memories, and she recalled the time when she'd joined him in the shower and helped lather him up. That scent had been ingrained into her memories as part of a very happy erotic, moment. Just inhaling it now was making her tingle in places that hadn't seen any action for quite a while now.

Which wasn't helpful.

Which was extremely frustrating!

'Call me when she starts to push,' he said.

'I will.' She watched him say goodbye to Sofia and Henry and then he was gone again. God, she missed that man! Missed being held by him, touched by him. Loved by him.

'That was your husband?' Sofia asked.

Grace nodded.

'Wow.'

Had he stopped loving her? Because she wasn't sure she'd ever stopped loving him, despite everything. Despite all the pain and the upset and the grief. Diego was going to be a hard habit to break. Would it get easier when she'd left Barcelona to go back home to England? Easier to know that he wouldn't be on the floor above her at work? Wouldn't be the on-call neonatologist? Wouldn't come swooping in to rescue other people's babies?

If she didn't see him every day—if they had distance between them and all that had happened—would that be simpler? They said absence made the heart grow fonder. She hoped that wasn't true. And when she'd been in Cornwall with Aunt Felicity she'd thought about Diego non-stop. Would he ever leave her heart?

She spent the next couple of hours concentrating on her patient, and when Sofia started to feel the urge to push she called Diego down.

He stood off to one side, just monitoring, waiting for Grace to deliver the baby.

Sofia pushed really well, and her husband Henry was a great coach.

'Come on, Sofia, you can do it! That's it! Yes! I can see the head!'

Sofia pushed with all her might, and after forty-five minutes of doing so baby Andrea burst into the world with a cry.

'Congratulations!' Grace said, clamping the cord as Andrea got his first cuddle with his mum. She looked up at Diego, smiling, happy. She couldn't help it. Every birth was special. Every healthy baby and healthy mother was a victory to her, and she wanted him to share her joy.

Eventually Diego took the baby to assess him, check his breathing, his reflexes, and pronounced him a healthy boy as he handed him back to his mother.

'No stitches!' said Grace. 'You're all good. Can I get you both anything? A drink?'

'Thank you,' Henry said, nodding.

'I'll just be a moment.'

Grace headed to the kitchenette, made them both a drink and some toast, took it to them and left the new parents to it.

Back at the midwives' desk, Diego waited for her. 'Do you want to get a coffee with me? I'm free now, if you want that chat.'

She nodded, suddenly nervous once again. 'I'll just tell Gabbi I'm going on my break.'

It felt strange to sit down with Grace at a table again. It had been a long time. When they'd lived together they'd tried to sit down and have meals with each other often, whether at home or at the hospital, snatched between shifts. It had been important to them that they stayed connected. Stayed present with one another.

He'd missed that. Having to sit in the hospital cafeteria alone felt awful, so Diego had often found himself dropping in on Zara if he stayed late at work and carried on into the morning. Zara seemed to like him dropping in at breakfast time to check on her.

'That was a good delivery,' he said, stirring milk into his coffee.

The cafeteria was mostly empty at night, and they sat alone in a booth by the back wall.

'Yes. It was. Sofia and Henry are lovely people. I really like them as a couple.'

'He's English?'

'Yes. A chef. He works here now.'

Diego nodded. 'But I don't think you asked to speak to me to talk about Henry's work. Is there something on your mind?'

He was dreading whatever it might be. Was this the point where she told him she was going to leave Spain? Or ask for a divorce? Neither of those was he ready for—though he assumed they were inevitable, after all the pain he'd caused her.

'There is.'

'Okay.' He tried to steel himself for it.

I want a divorce. I'm leaving.

'I've heard a rumour.'

'Oh?' That wasn't where he'd thought this conversation was going.

'About Isabella.'

Ah. Now he knew what this was about. He felt the muscles in his jaw tighten.

'She's seeing someone—an ER nurse?'

He nodded. 'Carlos.'

Now Grace nodded. 'I've met him a couple of times. He seems nice.'

Diego said nothing. Waiting.

'Is she pregnant, Diego?'

He looked away, down at his coffee, stirred it one more time even though he didn't need to. He'd dreaded this coming up, and knew he ought to have told her— but when could he have done so? When the words he was about to say would rip out her heart and cause her even more pain?

'Yes. She is.'

There was a terrible, dreadful pause as he saw all manner of emotions cross his wife's face.

'Why didn't you tell me?' she asked him, sounding hurt and betrayed.

The pain in her eyes tore through him and he felt ashamed and guilty. All he'd ever done was cause this woman pain, and here he was causing even more. He'd thought keeping the news from her was wrong, but he'd simply not known how to say anything.

'How could I? When would there have

been a good time to say it? Tell me.' He looked at her imploringly. 'I wanted to tell you. Believe me, this is not news I wanted to keep from you. But I didn't know what to say.'

'How long have you known?'

He sighed, knowing this would hurt her, too. 'Isabella told me when you were in Cornwall.'

Grace gasped, shocked.

Diego lowered his eyes, staring at his cup, unsure of what else to say. No matter what he did, no matter what he said, he always seemed to be in the wrong.

'Has it come to this? That we've ruined things between us so much we can't even tell each other the truth? That we walk on eggshells around each other?'

'I'm sorry. I've never meant to hurt you, Grace. Never.'

She stared back at him and took a big breath before sighing. 'Well, I hope it goes well for her. And maybe…just maybe…this can be a new beginning for the two of you. You've never seemed all that close. You have this great, huge family—you're so lucky— and yet you all seem so distant. Maybe this baby will bring you and Isabella closer.'

He wanted to reach out for her hand then. To lay his hand upon hers and thank her for being so...well, so graceful about all this. For thinking of him. For thinking of his relationship with his older sister when he knew that this news had to be hurting her.

'I can be happy for other women being pregnant, Diego. I can. I'm only hurt when people think they have to keep such good news from me. Am I so fragile that I have to be protected? Is that what people think?'

'You're the strongest woman I know,' he said, with an encouraging smile. 'After all that you've been through...you deserve your own happiness.'

He remembered when they'd met. How quickly he'd fallen in love with this remarkable woman who sat before him now. How Grace had accepted his proposal of marriage and how excited she'd been about the idea of a beach wedding in Spain with all his brothers and sisters. She'd been so excited to meet them and become a part of the Rivas family.

How disappointed she'd been to find out that they were not close, and when he'd managed to steer her towards a more sensible, more logical ceremony in London, with just a couple of colleagues as witnesses.

Was he fated always to disappoint her? To quash her dreams?

She smiled back. 'You're going to be an uncle.'

He nodded. Isabella would be the first of them to have a child, if all went well. 'And you're going to be an aunt.'

A strange look that he couldn't read passed over her face. There for a second, then gone.

'It's probably the closest I'll ever come to being a parent if…' Her voice trailed off.

'If what?'

'If we stay married.'

She was talking about them splitting up. Had she thought of that, then? Of leaving? Of divorcing him? He hoped not. He wasn't ready.

'What are you saying?' he asked.

'I'm just trying to be sensible, Diego. You left me. You moved out. We've agreed to tell people that it's over… Have you told anyone yet?'

He shook his head. 'No. Have you?'

'No.'

Well, that was good, at least. Or was it? Why exactly was he hanging on to this relationship when he knew in his heart of hearts that he had to let her go? When he had to give her the opportunity to find someone she could have babies with?

Because I still love her.

At that moment he wanted to take hold of her and hug her and kiss her, hold her tight and never let go! Show her just how much she still meant to him. But he knew he couldn't. It would be cruel. And so he sat with the pain and the discomfort of not being able to hold his wife. Of not being able to show her just how much she was still in his heart.

'I don't see how I will have any part in that child's life. I'm just trying to be sensible,' she said.

'You're its aunt. You will always be its aunt.'

At that moment her pager went off, and with reluctance he saw her look down at it.

'It's the ward. I'm being paged.' She pulled her mobile phone from her uniform pocket and called. 'It's Grace. What's up?'

He watched her face as she listened. Saw her go into work mode.

She put her phone away. 'It's the Garcia-Hernandez baby.'

'The spina bifida case?'

She nodded. 'It's here.'

* * *

Felicia Garcia-Hernandez and her husband Marcohad been coming into the hospital for regular scans ever since her baby's spina bifida was diagnosed. Grace had met with the couple numerous times before, and had even sat in on a consult with the couple, when they'd met Diego to discuss what treatment options their baby would need when he was born. She'd asked to be paged when they came in, and to be allowed in Theatre. As she stood scrubbing her hands and arms in the scrub room next to Diego she filled him in on what she'd been told.

'Apparently she went into labour just a couple of hours ago and gave birth in the car outside.'

'In the car park outside the hospital?' Diego asked.

She nodded. 'Ana was called out to the car. Felicia must have been terrified.'

'I'll bet.'

It felt good to be scrubbing in next to Diego. She had a focus—something else to think about after Diego's revelation about Isabella. She'd not been that surprised by the news. Rumours spread fast in hospitals, and they usually had an element of the truth to them. It was just the fact that he hadn't told her that upset her. But she had to be realistic. She had not made it easy for Diego to tell her about his sister. They'd hardly been talking to one another. They'd certainly not been having idle conversations allowing him to just drop it in casually.

Yet standing here now, side by side with him, something felt right, and she briefly wondered how many more of these occasions she would have with him. The thought made her sad. It felt wrong. They'd always made such a good team, and the thought of losing him completely...

I don't have to leave. I could stay.

But would that cause more issues in the long run?

If I stayed, would I have to watch Diego fall in love with someone else? Start a family with someone else?

She knew she would never be able to bear that. Despite everything that had happened she loved him. Deeply.

As they both walked through into Theatre nurses helped them don gloves and gowns, and they saw that baby Garcia-Hernandez was already prepped and anaesthetised on the table, face down, with only a small square of his lower back exposed, revealing the defect of an opening at the base of his spine, and a small sac containing nerves and membranes within.

Diego would operate to put the spinal cord and any exposed tissues and nerves back into the correct position and then close the gap, sealing the hole with muscle and skin. It wouldn't reverse any nerve damage. All he would be doing was repair work.

'Scalpel.' Diego held out his hand and the theatre nurse placed the blade in his hand so he could start.

Grace looked at Diego as he concentrated hard on the task at hand. His gaze was focused, determined. He worked methodically and carefully. Watching him was like watching the conductor of an orchestra. His movements were so sure and exact. Perfectly in control. The melody was of instruments and the procedure an exquisite choreography. The team knew what he needed even before he had to ask for it.

Diego was able to make such delicate surgery look easy. And watching him do the thing he'd been born to do…watching an expert—a maestro—at work… She could feel herself falling in love with him all over again.

Behind her mask she smiled as she looked at him, and in that exact moment he looked up and caught her doing so. He smiled back, his eyes creasing at the corners, and something between them changed in that moment. She wasn't sure what it was. Whether it was herself withdrawing from the battle lines, or whether it was something else. She didn't know, but she did know she didn't want to keep on fighting this man.

'Closing the dura now.'

The surgery had gone smoothly, as expected. She remembered something Diego had said to her when they'd first started going out. He'd come out of the theatre after performing a difficult foetal surgery, come over to her, smiling, and said, 'Every baby saved is a lifetime saved.' The words had struck her then, and they did so now.

Baby Garcia-Hernandez might still have a difficult road ahead of him, but at least he had a road. Her and Diego's babies had never had that chance. There had been no road, no path, not even a tiny muddy trail for them to go down. There had been no chance of a lifetime ahead of them. No going to school, no relationships, no finding their special someone. They'd had no idea how much they'd been loved and wanted and cherished. They'd never known. All that love only lived in her heart. And Diego's.

As they came out of surgery she looked at him and shook her head, smiling.

'What is it?' He smiled back, hands on hips, looking delicious and scrumptious, his hair slightly mussed from his scrub cap.

'You're amazing. I don't know if I ever told you enough, but…you are. What you're able to do in that room is unbelievable.'

Diego could do a great many things in many different rooms. The operating theatre was one. In the bedroom he was just as skilled, and by God she missed the feeling of his hands upon her body!

He looked down at the floor, still smiling, as if overwhelmed by her kind compliment. 'Thank you. I appreciate that.'

'It's the truth.' She laughed, suddenly feeling shy, suddenly feeling that this conversation would go in a direction that neither of them was ready for if she allowed it. Blushing, and feeling the heat in her cheeks, she decided that the best thing would be to create some space between them. At least for now.

'I...er... I'd better get back.' She met his gaze.

He was staring at her as if he was also fighting an internal battle. 'Okay.'

'I'll see you around.'

He nodded, backing away in the other direction, seeming reluctant to tear his gaze from hers. 'You most certainly will.'

Grace forced herself to turn and walk away—but, oh, goodness, it was so difficult!

What's happening? Were we flirting? We were flirting! We're not meant to be doing that!

But she couldn't stop smiling. Couldn't stop a small chuckle escaping. And when she allowed herself one last look over her shoulder as she reached the corner she saw that Diego was watching her go.

He smiled.

And her heart began to pound...

CHAPTER SIX

'WHY THE FROWN, Santiago?' Grace had stopped off at the cafeteria to grab a bowl of cereal for a patient when she'd seen him at one of the tables near the exit. Santiago was a paediatrician here at the hospital and one of Grace's good friends. 'Anything I can help with?'

He looked up at her and smiled. 'You're back! Did you have a good time in Cornwall?'

It had hardly been a good time. But she didn't want to tell him that. Especially since her relationship with Diego was now at a new and unknown stage, after they'd been in surgery with the Garcia-Hernandez baby.

'It was great. How are things with you?'

He shrugged. 'Frustrating. I've got a patient I'm having problems diagnosing. Her test results are mostly clear, but she's ill and I'm not sure what's wrong with her.'

At that moment another member of staff—Caitlin, the cardiothoracic surgeon who had sent Grace and Diego an invitation to their wedding in Maravilla—appeared beside them. 'Apologies, I don't mean to butt in, but I couldn't help but overhear what you said to Grace. I know an absolutely fabulous diagnostician called Elena who might be able to help you?'

Santiago looked up at her. 'Is she in this hospital?'

Caitlin shook her head. 'No. She's in Mallorca. But she's advised me on a couple of difficult cases before. I have her number, if you want it?'

He took a moment to consider it. 'Sounds great. All help is welcome on this one.'

Grace frowned. 'Do you mean Elena Solis? I think she's the lady who helped out with one of our patients, too.' She looked at Santiago. 'She's good. You ought to call her if you're stuck.'

Santiago smiled at both of them. 'I know when I'm beaten. Text me her number, Cait, when you have a spare moment.'

'I will. It's nice to have you back, Grace. We missed you!' And Caitlin went on her way.

Grace watched her go. Caitlin was at the beginning of all the fabulous adventures her life would hold. She was about to get married to Javier Torres, another cardiothoracic surgeon. They'd been reunited after Caitlin had been tasked to operate on Javier's sister. Quite the romance! And now their future was ahead of them.

Grace recalled how she'd missed out on the chance to plan her own wedding and make it the spectacular beach wedding she'd always wanted, whereas Caitlin was going to be married in the beautiful sprawling ancestral estate Maravilla, which belonged to Javier's family. She could only imagine how much fun Caitlin had had planning that…

There was much that Grace wished she had done differently. Even the happiness of having her big day had been denied her. But she'd been so keen to marry Diego and then fly with him to Barcelona to live and find work.

Why did it sometimes feel that life was happening to everyone else except for her? Why did she feel as if she was standing still?

'You okay?' Santiago asked.

She blinked, pulled back to the present, and smiled at Santiago. 'I'm fine.'

Diego had stopped by Grace's department. 'I've got an inguinal hernia to operate on. Want to join me?'

He looked down at her, once again taken by how much this woman was still a part of his life and how much she still meant to him. He was probably torturing himself by asking her, but he was still running on the high of their last conversation, when everything had gone so well and, like an addict, he needed more.

She nodded and said, 'Sounds great.'

He grinned. 'Ten minutes. Theatre two? It's Emilio Perez.'

'I'll be there. I'll just let Ana know where I'm heading.'

'Okay.'

He was inordinately thrilled that she'd agreed to join him. Something had changed in the last day or two between them. He didn't know when, exactly, or how—he just knew that he liked it. He liked the way she'd complimented him that day, and how she'd blushed when they'd flirted with one another.

There was nothing he liked more than to see her smile at him like that. He'd missed it. And now, incredibly, she was doing it again.

He wanted her back by his side in Theatre. Not so that she could admire him again, but because he *wanted* her there! Right now, they were getting on. The battle lines had been withdrawn and they were being friendly again—and by God he was grateful for that! At one point he'd thought he'd never be able to make her smile again. He'd never thought he had the right even to *try*. But she was smiling, and it was because of him, and he wanted to capture that feeling and hold it tight against him and never let it go.

So now she'd agreed to be with him in Theatre he almost skipped into the scrub room, and he still had a smile on his face when she joined him, to scrub in too.

'Hi.'

'Hi.'

She was already in scrubs, and was busy tying her hair up in a scrub cap decorated with unicorns. It was her favourite one.

She saw him look at it. 'You bought me this, remember?'

Of course he did. 'I do.'

She hit the water tap to get the water to

the right temperature and then opened up the small package from the dispenser that contained a nail brush, scrub sponge and nail pick. She laid it on the back of the sink, still in its packet, as she began to wet her hands and arms.

'Fill me in on the case?' she asked.

He liked this. They were good together. Not just at work, either.

'Baby Perez, born at thirty-nine weeks and two days, diagnosed with an inguinal hernia at birth. It was somehow missed on the ultrasound.'

'Was the baby born here? I don't recall seeing the name.'

'No. He was born at another local hospital but I've known the father of the baby for many years and he wanted me to do the surgery, so he brought the baby here.'

'Oh, okay… How old is he now?'

'A week.'

'And no other issues?'

'No, it should be relatively straightforward. And I thought after this maybe we could go and see Zara together?'

She smiled and nodded. 'Sounds good.'

'I've been checking in on her during the

day when I can, and she seems to be bearing up well.'

'You're not tired?'

'You know me.'

He winked at her without thinking, enjoying this simple conversation. This *ease* of conversation. The ability to just talk to Grace again as if the past hadn't happened. Could they carry on like this? Ignore the past and pretend that everything was all right? How long would that last?

The urge to take advantage of this moment and just lean in and kiss her was strong, and it physically pained him not to be able to do so. Instead, he concentrated on scrubbing, making sure he was thorough.

'Ready?'

She nodded. 'Ready.'

Grace watched him make a small incision so he could visualise the hernia. He easily separated the tissue sac containing the hernia from the cord structures, then opened it to look at the contents. Thankfully, it was empty. No bowel had slipped through and therefore there was no risk of strangulation.

'Straightforward…' she heard him mutter under his mask.

He inserted a laparoscope to check if there was herniation on the other side of the inguinal ring, but that was clear too. Next he tied off the sac with a suture, and removed the obsolete sac.

'Looks good,' she said.

He nodded. 'All that's left to do now is close up the incision.'

The relief in the room was palpable, as it always was after surgery on a baby. The fact that it had gone so well was reassuring, and she knew that Diego would be able to tell his friend that his son's surgery had gone perfectly.

She wanted to congratulate him. Before, whenever they'd been in surgery together and it had been a success, they would scrub out and she would give him a hug and a quick kiss. A kiss might be a step too far right now, but could she hug him? The desire to feel him in her arms again was dizzying...

But as they left Theatre a scrub nurse put her head around the door of the room and said, 'Are you guys looking after Zara Rodriguez?'

They both turned. 'Yes?'

'She's kind of upset. She's asking for you.'

'We'll be right there,' Grace said, before

turning to Diego. 'What do you think is wrong?'

'I don't know. She seemed fine the last time I saw her.'

They dried their hands with paper towels, threw the towels into the clinical waste bin, and then headed down to Maternity.

Grace felt a deep sense of unease in her stomach. Zara had been doing well these last few days. Her infection was gone, and she was putting on some weight now that she was getting regular meals and hydrating properly. What could have happened to upset her?

As they raced down to the ward Gabbi stopped Grace as she passed. 'We had a nightingale baby. Zara heard about it.'

Grace took in a breath and let it out again slowly. A nightingale baby was the name the staff gave to a baby that had been stillborn.

She knocked gently on Zara's door, with Diego close behind her. 'Zara? It's Grace and Diego.'

The door opened and Zara stood there crying, wiping her eyes with tissue. 'I heard her... I heard her, Grace!'

'Hey... Shh...' Grace led her back to her

bed, holding her hand. 'Tell me what happened.'

'Her baby—it…it died, and she was crying, and I've never heard anyone sound like that before, and…'

Grace swallowed hard. She didn't have to imagine what Zara had heard. She'd been there. She'd felt the raw, agonising pain that ripped through you when the baby they placed in your arms was lifeless. When you knew that baby would never open its eyes. When you knew that baby would never make a sound. When you held it, hoping beyond hope that some miracle would occur and it would begin breathing, only to realise with each passing second, each passing minute, that it would never, *ever* happen and that sweet, precious child would remain still.

The pain was like a volcano. A tsunami. An eruption. A wave of such grief and agony that there wasn't enough air, weren't enough words to describe what you feel when your very soul had cracked and shattered into tiny, fragile, broken pieces.

You'd stare at that baby in your arms, trying to absorb every detail of its face and its body through your own salty tears, through vision so blurred you were practically blind.

You'd hold on to your child. Not willing to let go, but knowing that at some point you must.

That pain was the worst.

Watching them take your child away and leave you with empty arms.

Grace herself had been through it. To know that there was a woman on this floor who was going through that hit right at her heart and ripped open old scars.

And for Zara to have heard that, knowing that her own baby was facing immediate surgery after birth…

'Hey, it's going to be okay,' she managed, the words sticking in her throat as it squeezed so tight she almost felt as if she couldn't breathe.

On this floor, in the Nightingale Suite, was a mother whose heart had been irreparably damaged for the rest of her life, and her instincts were to go to that woman and comfort her. Only she couldn't right now, because Zara needed her more in this moment. Grace knew that the other mother would have a dedicated bereavement midwife. Probably Ana. They'd all received training, but Ana specialised, as did Renata. That mother was being taken care of.

'It's just… I heard her crying… I was walking the corridor, trying to exercise a bit because I was having these cramps from sitting down so much. And now they're really beginning to hurt me and I'm afraid, Grace…afraid something is wrong.'

'Where are you having these cramps?' Diego asked gently.

'Down here.' Zara rubbed her abdomen just below her bump.

Grace looked at Diego, feeling the tears in her eyes, pleading with him to speak because she could not. She was still stuck in the past. Held there by remembered grief.

He understood. 'Let's put you on a trace. See if you're having contractions.'

'You think I might be in labour?' Zara asked, shocked.

'It's possible.'

She shook her head, adamant. 'No! I can't be! I'm not ready! What if he dies, Grace? I won't be able to handle it if he dies!'

Grace was so caught up in her own emotions at that moment that she still couldn't talk. Knew that if she did then she would cry herself.

Diego stepped forward. 'We're going to do our best not to let that happen. Okay?'

He turned to Grace. 'Why don't you go and fetch a trace machine?'

She nodded, grateful for the chance to escape the room, feeling her tears fall as the doors closed behind her and letting a deep, shuddering sob escape her as she stilled in the corridor.

Behind her, the door to Zara's room opened and closed again gently, and suddenly Diego's arms were around her and pulling her close.

It was something he'd hoped never to see again. That raw pain in his wife's eyes. Her reliving an experience neither of them would ever wish to go through again. It was as if they were right back there in the past, in their own birthing room.

He'd seen her try to be brave. Seen her try to stay strong for Zara, who herself was terrified and naturally so, but it had been too much, too soon, and his gaze had fallen on Grace as Zara had spoken, watching the crushing emotions silence her.

He'd known she needed to breathe. Needed a moment to gather herself. Known that Grace would be angry at not being able to control her emotions in front of her patient.

A patient who needed her to be strong. She hadn't wanted to fail Zara. So he'd suggested that Grace go and fetch a trace machine. That way she'd be able to escape the intensity of that room for a moment and gather herself.

But then, when she'd left, something inside him told him to follow her, and when he'd slipped into the corridor he'd found her, tears streaming down her face, and he'd just known he had to comfort her.

'Hey… I've got you. You're okay. It's okay.' He held her tight, stroking her hair, fighting back the painful lump of emotion welling in his throat.

Why did he feel as if he'd been thrown back in time? Why did this feel like the moment after they'd taken their baby boy away and Grace had looked so broken with no one in her arms to hold?

He carried the blame for that in his heart to this day.

Renata had told them to take as much time as they needed to be with their son. They had held him, cried over him, taken pictures, his handprint and footprint. Dressed him in an outfit that had been way too big for his tiny body and given him a little soft blue knitted hat. Then they'd spent ages just holding him and staring at him, telling him all about who they were and how much they loved him and how his family was going to miss him. Hoping still that a miracle would occur and he would start moving. Breathing. Would open his eyes. They'd stared at him with such intensity. It had seemed a crime to look elsewhere…he'd been that precious.

He'd never expected that. To stand in a delivery room looking down at his stillborn child. Who did? And he'd looked so perfect! As if nothing was wrong. So how could it have been so terribly wrong?

Hours had passed in that room and yet they'd only seemed like moments. Much too fleeting. Much too fast. And then he'd caught Renata's gaze through the small window on the door and she'd told him that they needed to come in. Needed to take their son away.

He'd known Grace wouldn't give him up and he'd known he'd have to separate them, even though it was the last thing that either of them wanted. He didn't want to lose Luca. This was his boy! His son! And he had failed him. Failed them both. Unable to protect either of them.

'Grace...it's time.'

She had ignored him. Pretending not to hear as she'd gazed down at their angelic little boy.

'Grace.'

'No,' she'd replied, not looking at him. *'No, it can't be.'*

'They need to take him.'

It hadn't been easy for him either. It hadn't been the way he'd imagined his journey towards having a large family of his own would go. He hadn't wanted to let him go either. But he'd known they couldn't keep Luca for ever, and that there were procedures the hospital needed to follow, and at some point they'd have to let him go.

Grace had shaken her head, tears dripping down onto Luca's shawl. *'No...'*

'Grace...'

He'd hoped his tone would tell her that he understood. He'd hoped that his voice would show her that this was impossible for him too, and that he was only trying to be sensible. He'd reached for his son. His wife had tried to hold on to him. She'd cried out, twisting away from him, trying to keep their son for a few precious moments more, sobbing, her tears dripping down onto his blanket.

And then she'd released him.

He'd scooped his son up, for the last time ever in his life, and looked into his tiny face, memorising those features one last time. Memorising the feel and weight of him in his arms. He'd kissed his son's forehead, trying to ignore the coolness of his body, whispered *'I love you...'* and then he'd taken Luca to the doorway, where Renata waited.

The midwife had taken Luca with reverence. Laid a hand on Diego's arm as a thank-you. *'We'll take good care of him. Now you two take good care of each other.'*

There had been tears in Renata's eyes, too.

He had nodded and turned back to Grace, but she had already pulled away from him, her cries into a pillow heart-rending. Each one slicing through his heart.

He had felt a piece of his soul disappear that day.

Now, as he stood in the corridor, Grace held tightly in his arms, he remembered his son's face.

'I'm sorry. I'm so sorry...' he whispered into his wife's hair, and waited for her sobbing to subside.

* * *

Her shift was nearly over. Technically, in ten minutes or so, Grace could go home. But Zara was in labour and she didn't want to leave her. The poor girl was scared, and Grace and Diego had promised to be by her side to get her through this.

'You're ten centimetres now. With the next contraction you can start pushing.'

Zara's labour had progressed well—and quickly, considering she was a first-time mum. Her contractions had come rapidly and had been strong enough to soften, shorten and dilate her cervix over only a few hours. She'd used gas and air, but had asked for an epidural when she'd got to about six centimetres, so that she could rest before pushing began.

'I'm scared.'

Grace gave her a smile. 'I know. But I'm here to look after you, and when your little boy gets here Diego will take care of him.'

'What if I can't do it?'

'Give birth?'

Zara nodded.

'You *can* do it. Whether he gets here naturally, or you have him another way, you *will* give birth to this baby.'

'And then he'll have to have surgery. That's no way to start a life.'

'But it will *save* his life. That's what matters.'

'You're so certain. So sure. You believe in medicine, don't you?'

'Don't you?'

Zara shook her head. 'Not always. My mum, she…she had breast cancer. She did everything right. Operations, medicines, chemo, radiation. Nothing helped her. No matter what the doctors did, she still died. That's why I never saw… I worry that…that the same thing will happen to my baby.'

'You just have to believe. What's the alternative?'

Zara nodded. 'I know. That's why it's so scary.'

'Trust me, your baby is in safe hands. And when he gets here you'll be putting him in the hands of the best neonatal surgeon I know.'

'You sound like you really believe in him.'

Grace nodded, feeling something warm and wonderful growing in her heart. 'I do.'

Zara smiled, nervous. 'Are you saying that because you really believe it, or because he's your husband?'

'The first one.' She smiled back. 'He's a good man, Zara. The best. He knows what this means. He knows how scared people are, putting their brand-new babies into a surgeon's hands. He doesn't take that lightly. He's careful, and talented, and if I were in your place I would want Diego to take care of my child.'

'Do you have kids?'

How to answer? Tell Zara that they'd had three and lost every single one? When she was trying to convince her patient that Diego was the best person to look after her baby?

'No, not yet.'

Grace had her hand on Zara's bump and felt it hardening. She was grateful for the diversion.

'Okay, here's a contraction. I want you to take a big breath, curl up and bear down— like you're having a big bowel movement.'

Zara sucked in a breath and began to push.

Grace tried not to think of her three babies. What it might have been like to be a mother of three. She was acutely aware of their due dates and marked each one with a little candle and a whispered, *I will love you for ever.* She'd thought she was the only one to suffer their loss so openly. Diego had been distant. Buried under work. Barely at home. She'd not felt that she could reach out to him for his support.

Until today.

Today, Diego had held her as she cried.

Today, Diego had shown her that he was there for her and that her pain was a burden he also carried.

She'd never suffered alone. She'd just thought she had.

But what did this mean for them, as their relationship stood now?

Wrapped in her husband's arms, her head against his chest, listening to the steady and sure beat of his heart, she had felt so comfortable. As if she was home again. Safe. Relaxed. Cared for. *Loved.*

Was there still a future for them? Was there still hope?

'And again. Deep breath—and push!'

Zara was pushing as well as she could, but sometimes it was difficult to push with an epidural still in full effect. A woman couldn't always tell if she was pushing in the right way.

'Well done. Okay, take a rest. Do you need some water?'

Zara nodded, and Grace held a cup up to her mouth.

Behind them, the door opened and Diego came in. 'How's she doing?'

'She's started pushing.'

'Excellent.' He went to the other side of Zara's bed and picked up a small flannel, used it to wipe Zara's face.

Grace smiled at the gesture. He was so kind. So thoughtful. Had she misjudged him? Had she been too abrupt? She didn't want to throw away her marriage. She didn't really want to leave Barcelona and return to England. This was her home now. These people, this country—she loved them all. And she still loved Diego. How could she not? He held such a big part of her heart.

Okay, so maybe they'd had a difficult year or two. The stress of losing three babies would test any marriage. It was what you did afterwards that counted. And perhaps neither of them had acted reasonably? He'd distanced himself from it all. Who was to say that was the wrong way to deal with grief?

I distanced myself from him. Maybe that was wrong, too?

All she knew in that moment was that she

had to try. Had to try and get things back on a steady footing between the two of them. Had to let him know, somehow, that she was willing to give things a go if he still wanted her.

Did he still want her? That was the big question.

'Okay, here comes another contraction now. Big push!'

Zara groaned and bore down hard.

'I can see hair!' Grace smiled, looking up and meeting Diego's gaze.

He smiled back at her, and she could see that he wasn't just smiling at her because of the magical event happening in the room—he was smiling at a woman he loved still.

She felt sure of it.

'And again! Come on, you can do it!'

Zara pushed again and again and again, and finally, after claiming she had nothing left, she gave one last push and the head was out.

'Reach down, Zara. Feel your baby.'

She did, and a hesitant smile crept across her face. 'It's him!'

'Yes, it is. One last push and he's going to be here.'

Diego was ready with the incubator. Ready to take the baby and whisk him away.

Zara gave one last, strenuous push, and with a large gush of hind waters Baby Rodriguez was born, straight onto his mother's tummy, with a loud cry.

'Oh, my God!' Zara cried. 'He's here! Is he okay?'

'You hear that crying? He's okay!' Grace attached two clamps and cut the cord in between them. She used a towel to rub him down and get him dry. She was feeling optimistic. He was a good size. At least seven pounds. And although his exomphalos was sizeable, it was still neatly contained in its sac.

'Has he got a name?' she asked.

Zara shook her head. 'I didn't want to choose one. In case he…'

Grace understood. 'He's here now. You should think of a name for him. He's real. He has a birthday. Now he needs a name.' She knew how important that was. Even for the babies you lost.

'Give him a hug and a kiss, Zara. Because I need to take him,' said Diego.

'So soon?' Zara looked scared.

'He needs to be able to feed.'

Zara nodded, then she kissed the top of his head and whispered something to him that neither Grace nor Diego caught.

'Okay. I'm ready.'

Diego came forward and scooped him up gently. 'I'll take extra-special care with this young man, okay?'

Zara nodded, smiling through her tears. 'Make sure that you do.'

'I'll treat him like he's my own.'

Grace met his gaze then, feeling her heart caught in her throat, wishing she could say something. Wishing she could ask him what he was feeling. But he was gone, Zara was sobbing, and right now her patient needed her more than Grace needed to know what was happening between herself and her husband.

So she turned back to her, smiling as she checked on Zara's bleeding. 'He's in the best hands. So let's get you strong enough to look after him when he comes out of surgery.'

'How long will it take?'

'A few hours.'

Zara let out a heavy sigh and wiped her eyes.

Grace examined her and discovered she had a second-degree tear. 'You're going to need a stitch or two once you've delivered the placenta.'

'Okay.'

It was as if Zara was steeling herself. Or detaching herself. Grace couldn't tell.

Her placenta was delivered easily, and in one reassuring piece.

'Your epidural is still working, so I don't need to give you a local. You shouldn't feel this.'

The tear had ripped through the skin and muscle of Zara's perineum and extended slightly inwards. She would need at least five stitches, by Grace's judgement.

'Let me know if you do feel anything.'

Grace stitched carefully. Normally, new mothers didn't notice this part. They were too busy cuddling their babies or celebrating with their partners and taking photos. But Zara had no one with her, and her son was with Diego now, being prepped for surgery, and she just stared up at the ceiling, her face devoid of emotion.

'When your epidural wears off you shouldn't feel the stitches, really. Only a small amount of discomfort. And they'll dissolve on their own, so no need to come in to have them removed.'

'Mm-hmm.'

'We usually recommend that you don't have intercourse for four to six weeks. Until you're completely healed.' She was hoping that Zara would engage with her. Answer her. But she was getting nothing. Was this how Diego had felt, trying to talk to her after their losses?

'If you do feel anything you should apply a cold pack wrapped in a towel, but if the pain gets bad, or you think there might be an infection, then come back in and see us, okay?'

Zara nodded, her gaze still fixed on the ceiling.

Grace didn't like the way Zara was distancing herself. It hit too close to home. Had she done this? To Diego?

Yes, I did. But how hard did he try to reach me?

She remembered him sitting at the end of her hospital bed, trying to talk to her. How he'd kept saying her name, and how she'd not acknowledged him or spoken to him because she'd been feeling so awful, so terrible, that she couldn't carry a baby to term. How useless she'd felt. How guilty for trapping her husband with her, a woman incapable of giving him the family he deserved. How angry she'd been that he'd forced Luca from her arms and taken him away, leaving her with empty hands and a broken heart.

She'd not felt worthy of his love and affection and so she'd withdrawn. Ignored all attempts to engage with her. She'd been like Zara.

Grace cleared away her equipment, washed her hands, and then sat down beside Zara on her bed. She reached for her patient's hand and squeezed it. 'I'll wait with you. You're not alone in this—you hear me? You're not alone.'

A solitary tear trickled down Zara's face.

CHAPTER SEVEN

THE SURGERY WAS more complicated than Diego had expected.

There was a lot of swelling around the baby's exomphalos, and he wasn't able to reduce it as much as he wanted. He had to leave the sac in a silo. He fixed the throat issue, so that Zara's baby would be able to feed, but the baby's blood pressure kept crashing, and at one point his heart actually stopped. It was touch and go, and Diego's nerves were on edge. He knew this baby needed to rest and recover before it could have any more surgery, and he was glad Grace wasn't there to watch.

'Let's get him up to the NICU. I want half-hourly obs.'

'Yes, Doctor.'

He took off his gown and gloves and scrubbed out before heading out into the corridor and down to the maternity floor to speak to Zara and Grace. Exhaustion swamped him. He hadn't slept much during the day, his mind filled with what was happening between him and his wife and where they were headed. It was all he could think about these days. Now he needed a break. Things had been so intense for so long.

At Zara's room, he knocked on the door and went in.

Grace was sitting by Zara's bed, looking half asleep, but she woke up when she saw him. 'How did it go?' she asked.

'He's all right. He's in the NICU, Zara, so you can go up and visit him when Grace says you're ready.'

'And he's fixed? It's all done?' Zara asked in a low voice that betrayed no emotion. It was as if she was cautious about hearing his answer.

'I've fixed the fistula in his throat and joined the two ends, but there was some swelling in the abdomen and I was unable to reduce the exomphalos. I've placed it in a silo, and hope to reduce it when the swelling goes down.'

'What does that mean? That his organs are still on the outside of his body?'

'Yes. But only for the next day or so. We can go in again and reduce them further... maybe sew him up completely.'

'You mean he'll need further surgery?'

'Yes.'

'You told me you'd fix him.'

'I know, but these situations are all individual. As I said, there was too much swelling to—'

Zara held up her hand, silencing him. 'When can I go and see him?'

Grace glanced at her. 'I can get you a wheelchair and take you.'

'Now?'

She nodded. 'Now.'

Grace followed Diego out of the room, closing it softly behind her. 'Tricky case, huh?'

He felt frustrated. He'd almost promised this young woman that he'd work miracles and fix her baby. Why had he done that? Was it because Grace was involved?

'Yeah. But it happens...you know that.'

'I do. I'll talk to her—don't worry.'

'Thanks.'

'Are you okay?'

He looked at her. Looked into the beautiful blue eyes that were looking at him with such concern right now. He knew that she understood what he was feeling and he was grateful for it. Grateful to her for asking.

'I'm okay. You?'

She smiled back. 'I'm okay too.'

The machines created a reassuring rhythm and a musicality that was almost soothing. At least it was to Grace. For Zara, seeing her baby lying in an incubator, covered in wires and tubes and sensors, his intestines visible in the silo pouch, it must be terrifying. To her it would look unreal, as if some kind of awful nightmare was happening to her baby, right before her very eyes.

She burst into tears on seeing him, only stopping when Grace suggested she wash her hands and use the access panels to reach through into the incubator and touch him. Hold his hand and speak to him.

'Let him know that you're here,' she told her.

Grace's shift had been over long ago. Daylight was streaming in through the windows. But she knew she couldn't go yet. Zara needed her. And so she sat with the new mother and her baby for quite a while, before suggesting that Zara go back to her room to try and sleep.

'He'll be looked after…don't worry. If there's any problem someone will come and get you.'

'Will you be watching him?'

'It's really Diego's department rather than mine.'

Grace wheeled Zara back to her room and got her settled, then left her to get some rest. Then she headed back into the corridor and let out a big sigh. She was exhausted.

'Grace? You're still here?'

Diego's voice came from her left and she turned to see her husband striding towards her in casual clothes, a backpack slung over his shoulder. He looked good.

'I'm about to leave now. Zara's trying to get some rest.'

'You look shattered. Have you eaten?'

'No. I'll probably grab something on the way home. I don't think I've got the energy to cook.'

'Let me take you out for breakfast.'

She felt her heart accelerate. She couldn't remember the last time she'd eaten breakfast with Diego. But was it the right thing to do? Would she just be torturing herself with memories of how things used to be? However, she was so exhausted she decided to go with it. Besides, they'd been getting on so much better just lately.

'That'll be nice. Thanks. Give me two minutes to get changed?'

'I'll wait outside.'

Grace smiled. 'I won't be long.'

She felt as if she was back on her very first date with Diego. Only this time, instead of walking through the dark streets of London on their way to a show, they were walking through the brightly lit streets of Barcelona, with the hot morning sun beaming down upon their shoulders.

'How's Isabella?' she asked tentatively.

'She's well, as far as I know.'

'You haven't spoken to her lately?'

He shrugged. 'I've been kind of busy.'

She nodded. 'Zara told me you've been visiting her during the day. Have you been getting much sleep?'

Another shrug. 'You know me...'

Yes. She did. When he was worrying about things he worked. Long, hard hours. More than he should, putting himself last.

'You need to take care of yourself.'

'I know.' He smiled.

'How can you give your best to your patients if you're exhausted?'

'Is this wifely concern?'

She laughed. 'If it's still allowed.'

'It is.'

She nodded, smiling to herself, glad that he still considered her his wife. 'I'm serious, though. You can't burn the candle at both ends. You can't do nights and work during the day, too. Mistakes might happen.'

'I know. And now that Zara's baby is born I'll stop checking in on her during the day— how about that?'

'That sounds good. And no checking in on anyone else either. You must rest.'

'Yes, ma'am.'

She nudged him playfully with her elbow. 'I'm serious!'

He laughed. 'I know. I'm just kidding with you.'

They walked a little further, comfortable in the silence, not feeling compelled to fill it. It was nice to be with Diego again this way. She'd missed it. Missed *him*. Incredibly so.

'Still hungry?'

'Starving. I don't think I grabbed a bite all night.'

'Fancy heading over to La Casa?'

La Casa. Their place. Their special break-fast spot.

She looked him in the eye. 'I'd love that. Yes.'

'Okay. Let's go.'

Normally she would reach for his hand as they walked, but she wasn't sure what the etiquette was for that now. So instead she fiddled with the strap of the bag that crossed her chest, occasionally risking a glance at Diego, admiring his profile, wondering how she'd ever got so lucky as to have this man fall in love with her and marry her.

Was he thinking about touching her the way she was thinking about touching him? When had she last let her fingers trail across his chest? When had she last touched him intimately? She knew every inch of him, and that was probably why she was finding it so hard only having her bag strap to fiddle with!

She wanted to reach out. Take hold of his hand. Feel his skin pressed against hers. Lay her head against his shoulder and stroke his arm. Feel his muscles. The solidity of his body. His quiet strength. To inhale him. Feel the brush of his stubble against her face. And so much more.

Her body was coming alive. She was next to him, away from the hospital, no longer hidden behind the barriers of work and her uniform. Their dedication to their patients had been taken away for now and they were in the open again. The possibilities were endless.

When they reached La Casa, Diego pushed open the door, holding it for her to go through first, and as soon as they stepped over the threshold, with the little bell above the door announcing their arrival, she heard the familiar voice of Felipe, the owner.

'Grace! Diego! My favourite couple! Where have you been? It's been so long!' Felipe clapped Diego on the back as he gave him a hug and then he reached for Grace's hand and raised it to his lips, kissing the back of it.

'Hello, Felipe.'

'Would you like your favourite table?'

'Yes, please.'

'This way.' He beamed, as if he was genuinely thrilled to see them, and Grace looked at Diego and they smiled at each other. They had always come to La Casa for breakfast if they'd both been on a night shift. Always ordered the same thing. It was a ritual they'd created in their marriage.

'Their' table was out at the back, in La Casa's rear garden. They liked it there because after a busy nightshift neither of them had any need to be surrounded by people. They liked the quiet and the privacy and the beautiful flower-filled terrace Felipe had created out there.

There were pots and baskets of geraniums and jasmine, ivy, bougainvillea and lilies. A large stone fairy in mid-flight reached out a hand, her fingertips caught in the water from a water feature that cascaded down various levels of slate and stone. Above, there were lanterns of many colours. It was the perfect spot. One they cherished.

Diego held out a chair for her and she sat down. Felipe laid her serviette in her lap with a grand flourish, almost as if they were in a Michelin-starred restaurant, before he poured water into their glasses.

'Would you like the menu, or should I just prepare your favourites?'

Grace looked at Diego.

'The usual, please, Felipe.' Diego smiled.

'Perfect. I'll have José bring out the coffee.'

'Thanks.'

'We haven't been here in ages. I bet he wondered what had happened to us.'

'I think we all probably wondered that,' Diego said, looking at her with a regretful smile.

She nodded. What could she say? At the time neither of them had known what was happening. Neither of them had known the implications for their marriage. The damage they were doing. They'd each just been trying to get through the day the best way they knew how.

When she'd had the miscarriages, when she'd lost the baby, the world had paused for her and Diego, but it had carried on for everyone else. The only way she could describe it was like a scene in a film where one person stood still and all around the world whizzed by so fast it was a blur. But they weren't still now. Were they?

'How do you see us now?' she asked, nervous about his answer.

He let out a breath, smiled. 'I think I like the fact that we can talk now. I've missed you, Grace.'

The last time he'd told her he missed her she'd berated him. Told him he had no right to say that to her. But this time she appreciated it more than she could say. She felt her heart swell with gratitude and happiness.

'I've missed you, too.' Her voice broke slightly on the last word and she felt her cheeks colour with heat.

The walls between them were coming down and that was good! Because if they could keep going in this direction then maybe something from this relationship could be saved? Whether that something was an actual future or not she couldn't know, but she liked what she was hearing. What she was feeling towards him.

People made mistakes. She might have felt that had Diego withdrawn from her and let her down once upon a time—but what had she done to him?

I'm not perfect. I've made mistakes, too. The solution is to learn from those mistakes, and maybe that's what we're doing right now.

'Here you go…' Felipe arrived at their table with a tray and a big smile upon his face. '*Torrada amb tomàquet* and *punxo de truita*. Enjoy!'

'Thank you, Felipe. This looks amazing—as always.'

She felt her mouth water at the sight, and at the aromas currently filling her nostrils. The sourdough toast was perfectly crisped, the rich red of the tomatoes was speckled with black pepper, and the omelette was rich with crisp potatoes. Hot steam was rising, urging them to eat at once.

Felipe disappeared like a magician and they both grabbed their cutlery, keen to tuck in and eat, to refuel after a long night shift of looking after Zara, delivering her baby and performing surgery.

The food was just as they remembered. If not better. It provoked memories of happier times, before their world had collapsed into ruin. Being here at La Casa, sitting opposite one another, eating the food they'd always eaten, looking into one another's eyes...

'Thank you for asking me to come here, Diego.'

'Who else would I bring to La Casa?'

She smiled. 'You know what I mean.'

'I do. Thank you for saying yes.'

'I wouldn't have missed this.'

They ate companionably, occasionally meeting each other's gaze and giving a warm, loving smile. Eventually their conversation turned to chit-chat about their friends at work, the cases they'd worked on, and towards the end of their meal Grace spoke of how Aunt Felicity had been when she had gone back to England.

Felipe took away their empty plates and returned with *churros* covered in cinnamon and icing sugar as their dessert. Grace wasn't sure she'd be able to eat anything else, but she couldn't resist at least one. And when they paid they hugged Felipe and promised they'd be back again soon, then headed out onto the streets of Barcelona.

It was busier. Filling up with tourists and locals. They walked through the market, casually stopping to look at stalls that caught their interest, and on through the streets to the beautiful Basilica de la Sagrada Familia—a towering masterpiece of gothic construction, resplendent with ornate stonework and filigreed spires and steeples.

Grace sighed. 'It's so beautiful… I can't remember ever having looked at it so carefully, and yet I must have passed it dozens of times since I've been here.'

'I think we're all guilty of not seeing the beauty of something that's right before us day after day,' said Diego. 'We take it for granted.'

She nodded. 'I think you're right.'

She knew she'd begun to take Diego for granted—expecting him to be there, expecting him to support her no matter what, so that when he'd been unable to she'd got angry with him, not allowing him the respite of understanding that he was hurting too.

They passed around to the Passion Façade. This side of the basilica was plain and simple, carved with harsh lines that she'd once been told represented the bones of a skeleton, to strike fear into the onlooker. She thought about the beauty of this place, how even something so wonderful had a dark side to it. Pain. Grief.

Maybe everything did?

'Do you want to go inside?' Diego asked.

'Yes.'

He reached out and took her hand in his, surprising her. But she looked down at their entwined hands and smiled, and allowed him to lead her inside.

It was immediately cooler, and once her eyes had adjusted from the bright sunshine outside she looked up and gasped. The vaulted ceiling was the most incredible thing she had ever seen! Tall white columns rose up like flawless birches, and the ceiling looked like a collection of carved white flowers, each with a dark heart. Either side of them, along the walls, were windows of stained glass. All the colours shone down upon those inside, inspiring awe and moments of reflection. It truly was a building in which to just stop and breathe and take a moment to appreciate the wonder of life.

By the altar was an area where people could light a candle. Grace took a taper and lit four of them.

Diego looked at her. 'Four?'

'One for each of our babies and one for us.'

He smiled at her and raised her hand to kiss the back of it, the way Felipe had. But unlike Felipe's kiss this one meant something. Despite the beauty of her surroundings, the awe that it inspired, all Grace could think of was that kiss. The feel of his lips upon her skin and the way he'd looked into her eyes as he'd kissed her.

Something was happening here. Something was changing between them and she was ready for it! She was so happy that they were moving forward, past the pain of the last couple of years, past the hurt and the grief. Here they were reconnecting, rediscovering all that they'd felt for one another!

This was something they could get past. This was something they would conquer! She felt it deep in her bones and in her heart and her soul. She felt her heart quicken, her pulse thrum, as the sweet anticipation of Diego's kiss woke every nerve-ending in her body.

She wanted him. Wanted, in that moment, to forget all their pain, forget all their mistakes and just take Diego home and enjoy his body the way she always had.

But they were in the basilica, and their apartment was a few miles away. A good walk unless they caught a taxi. Right now she'd just have to accept what was happening and allow the anticipation of later to wait.

They spent a good thirty minutes in the basilica and then headed back outside into the morning heat, towards the Plaça de la Sagrada Família—a beautiful tree-lined square filled with walkways and benches. It was packed with people. A lot of them were tourists, trying to get some good photographs of the basilica.

Grace and Diego walked past them all slowly, as if neither of them wanted their time together to end.

Diego had so much he wanted to say, but all the speeches and words he kept practising in his mind over and over again seemed inadequate for what he wanted to express. He was very much a man of action, and though he wanted so much to be able to say to Grace that he was treasuring this moment, he didn't want her to think that it was going somewhere it could never go. No matter how much they bonded again, and no matter how much they pretended that the past didn't exist, it did. And dining together, holding hands, lighting candles and spending time together, did not wipe out a past filled with pain and grief.

And yet...

He felt the lure of it. The desire, the temptation to ignore the past. This moment that they were sharing right now was just so wonderful, so hypnotic. Like a mirage promising a better life. A new way to be together.

It's easy, it seemed to say. *Just do this.*

He so much wanted to live in this moment. To just be present and forget the past, ig-

nore the possible future. To revel in this gift
he was being given of time with Grace and
being kind and loving to one another again.
When he'd taken her hand he'd done so without thinking about what he was doing. It had
been natural. He'd forgotten they were split
apart. He'd forgotten the arguments and the
hurt. He'd just taken her hand in his and
acted as if it was the most natural thing in
the world for him to do. As it had been once
upon a time.

'I should walk you home. I've kept you up
far too long,' he said.

Grace nodded and they walked companionably side by side, in no great hurry.

He didn't want to think about getting
back to the apartment they'd once shared.
He didn't want to think about that moment
when she'd disappear inside and leave him
outside. That part was going to be hard. Because he wanted to continue to live in this
fantasy land where he and Grace were partners again.

As they passed a flower seller he bought
a small bunch of flowers and gave them to
her. She held them to her nose and inhaled
their scent, smiling, and then she went up
on tiptoe and kissed his cheek.

He almost froze when she did so. Knowing she was going to kiss him. Feeling the press of her soft lips against his face. Closing his eyes to treasure every nanosecond of it.

But then she was gone again, back to walking alongside him, and the kiss was over. And yet it was all he could think about. Her lips. Her mouth. Her tongue. Dear God, when was the last time they'd kissed? Passionately? Just thinking about it, he could remember how she'd tasted, how she would feel in his arms, and his body sprang to life, making it awkward for him to walk as they continued across the city towards their home.

He struggled for something to say. Struggled to think of a safe topic to talk about so as not to ruin the moment. In the end, he decided on silence. Her hand was still in his and that would have to be enough for him—though occasionally he was aware of her lifting the flowers to her nose, and one time she rested her head against his shoulder.

He wanted to rest his head on top of hers. Or maybe even reach up and stroke her hair, but if he did…

I'd want so much more! And I cannot in good conscience take any more from this woman who has already suffered too much because of me!

His mouth felt dry. His heart pounded in his chest painfully. Every step was a torture, when all he wanted to do was stop, turn and face her, and kiss her like there was no tomorrow.

They reached the street where he'd used to live with her and he felt his steps slow. He was not yet willing to give up this precious time. He wanted to eke it out for as long as he could. Because once he said goodbye, once he let her go and she went inside alone, the spell would be broken and they would go back to being colleagues again. Would they ever recapture the magic of this moment?

He gazed up at the window, saw the flower pots on the balcony, remembered how sometimes they would sit outside in the morning and share breakfast before work. The wrought-iron table and chairs were still there, with the bright red cushions still on the seats. He remembered how one morning they'd been sitting out there and Grace had used her foot under the table to stroke his leg, whilst staring intently at him…how he'd not been able to concentrate before she'd finally reached over, taken his hand in hers and led him into the bedroom.

They'd been so good together!

How had it all fallen apart?

'Well, this is me,' Grace said as they came to a stop outside the apartment door. It was still painted green and the paint was still peeling. He'd meant to redo it but never got around to it. Another failure of his.

'Yes. Thanks again for joining me for breakfast. It was good to spend time with you again.'

She nodded. 'It's been nice.'

She smiled back at him almost shyly, as if this truly were some first date and he'd walked her back to her door. And now there would be that awkward moment where you never quite knew if a kiss would be welcomed. And if you did go in for one should it be a kiss on the cheek? Or something more daring?

'So, I guess I'll see you tonight? At work? You'll check in on Zara's baby?'

'I'll bring her up to visit him, yes.'

'That's great.'

God, he wanted to kiss her so badly! He felt that if he could kiss her just once then it would get it out of his system... But he wasn't sure he'd have the strength to stop at a simple kiss. He'd want it to be so much more and then what would happen? But if he walked away without kissing her…he'd feel awful! He'd feel he was disappointing her again.

Because right now she was looking up at him as if she was waiting for a kiss.

And how could he refuse her that?

Diego swallowed hard, then leaned in for a goodbye kiss on the cheek. He figured that would be the safest bet. They would both get what they wanted, he wouldn't be rude, just walking away, and a peck on the cheek would be simpler than anything else.

But as he leaned in and pressed his lips against her cheek he found himself lingering, inhaling the scent of her—soap, and a faint perfume that he couldn't identify. Something floral, heavenly. He felt her turn her face to his lips, as if she was savouring the feel of his mouth upon her skin, and he pulled back slightly and met her gaze.

Those blue eyes of hers…so soft, so alluring…were darkened with arousal as she gazed at him and something happened in him. Something he couldn't describe… something he didn't want to think about too much. He just knew he had to kiss her properly.

He brought his lips close to hers, looked one last time into her eyes, aware that she was breathing heavily, and felt a jolt of lust hit him low and hard.

And then he kissed her.

Grace had thought he wasn't going to kiss her goodbye. She'd sensed his hesitation and even understood it. If he kissed her on the mouth it would signal a direction for their relationship that neither of them could possibly be sure of. They'd broken up. He'd moved out. She'd thought it was over. And now they'd had such a great nightshift together, a wonderful breakfast, an amazing walk around Barcelona... They were talking, enjoying each other's company again, laughing, living in the moment and remembering what had been so good between them.

If he kissed her and meant it, then... Well, she wasn't sure what that would signify. All she did know was that she wanted him to do it. So when he'd leaned in and pressed his lips against her cheek she'd pressed her face into them, enjoying that brief moment of feeling his stubble against her face, the rasp of his whiskers against her cheek, and she'd closed her eyes at the rapturous pleasure of knowing that her Diego, her *darling* Diego, was kissing her once again.

Maybe it would be the last time? Maybe this was it? A goodbye kiss? And if it was she wanted it to last and last, for ever and ever, because it felt so good to have him this close once again.

And then he'd hesitated, and she'd opened her eyes to look into dark chocolate pools, and she'd just known that this was no longer going to be a peck on the cheek. This was about to become something more. And she'd welcomed it, wanted it. Wanted *him*!

When his lips pressed against hers, softly at first, and his hands cradled her face, she felt herself sink against him, surrendering to whatever happened. His tongue began to explore her mouth and she met it with her own, entwining them, tasting him, letting their kiss become deeper and deeper and more passionate.

She let out a soft groan, her breathing heavy as they stood there in the middle of the street kissing, her hands grasping at his body, touching him, wanting more, wanting to rip off his shirt and feel his bare flesh, but restraining herself.

It was as if they couldn't get enough of each other and the tension of the last few weeks was exploding out of them as they rediscovered each other after so long apart.

And then, with his hands in her hair, he broke apart from her, breathing heavily, his eyes dark as he gazed at her, breathing heavily.

'Come upstairs with me, Diego,' she said, her intention clear.

They could build on this. They could move forward. If they could get over this, they could get over anything. She knew they had it in them.

She felt him let go of her hair and he took a step back, suddenly looking around him, as if remembering they were in public. She could see that he was aroused, and it pleased her, but what didn't please her was the look on his face.

'I'm sorry. I shouldn't have... I wasn't thinking.'

'Neither was I.' She smiled. 'Come home with me.'

He took another step back, shaking his

head, checking his watch. 'I can't. I…er… need to go back to the hospital.'

'Diego—'

He held up both his hands, palms outward, as if placating her. 'I'm so sorry.'

And he turned and walked away from her.

Grace watched him go, her heart breaking.

How could she have misread the situation so badly? She'd thought he wanted the same thing. She thought that he wanted her back.

Only he didn't.

Perhaps that *had* been a goodbye kiss after all?

Diego forced himself to walk away, fighting the tremendous urge he felt to simply turn around, rush straight back into her arms and take her upstairs and ravish her the way his body wanted.

Only he couldn't.

And she would never know the strength it took him to keep creating distance between them. He couldn't wait to get to the end of the street so that he could stop and breathe and gather his will and his composure.

Kissing Grace had been like…heaven.

Kissing Grace had been everything he'd wanted.

The way she made him feel…the way she made him yearn for her…it was killing him! But he had to walk away. Had to be logical and sensible and ignore everything that his heart and body was screaming at him and instead listen to his head, remember just how complicated they would make things if they became intimate with each other again.

Because although it might have been wonderfully magical to enjoy her kiss and remind himself of everything about her that he loved, it would, in the end, have done neither of them any good at all.

Nothing had changed. Nothing had been resolved. They would have just become stuck again. Stuck in a relationship with major problems that they still needed to talk about.

When he'd written that note about moving out, he'd said *For now.* He'd thought a break apart would do them both good. But then somehow Grace had come back from Cornwall and told him that they needed to tell everyone it was over between them. He'd assumed she'd made her choice. He couldn't give her the family she desired so she'd ended it. He couldn't comfort her because she would never allow it. He couldn't talk to her because…well, because he hadn't been ready. He hadn't known what to say. But their time apart had given him the space he'd needed to formulate his thoughts.

They needed to talk to one another before they did anything else, and if he'd gone up those stairs with her the only language they'd have been expressing would have been bodily. Sexually. Intimately. Emotionally.

And even though his body wanted that, he wasn't interested in just scratching an itch. Grace deserved better than that—and so did he.

Going upstairs to the apartment together might have seemed like a step forward for them, only it wouldn't have been. It would have been a sticking plaster on a gaping wound that was still gushing blood profusely. They'd not fixed things between them. Yes, he could have been greedy and sated himself with her body, but that would have been wrong. Especially when she'd soon have realised they were still in the same situation and the arguments would have begun again.

He couldn't face that. He wouldn't use her.

Walking away from her before she left for Cornwall had almost killed him.

Walking away now…?
He could barely breathe.
But it was the only sane thing to do.
And maybe one day she would understand.

CHAPTER EIGHT

THE NEXT NIGHT Grace sat at the midwives' desk, twirling her pen and staring off into space instead of writing up notes as she was meant to be doing.

She just couldn't concentrate! She'd even considered taking a night off and not coming in, but the night shifts were already understaffed, and Renata had begged her to work them. She couldn't let others down. Not her friends and colleagues, nor her patients.

But she was alert to any new people coming onto the ward. Alert for Diego.

What would they say to each other after this morning?

That kiss. That kiss had been everything. *Everything!* Grace had kissed her husband as passionately as he had kissed her, and had stupidly believed—naively or not—that it meant a turning point for them. That they were moving forward and there didn't have to be a separation or the breakdown of their marriage. That there was still enough between them to work it out.

It had taken a lot of courage to ask him up to the apartment. To blatantly ask him to stay with the implication that it would lead to sex. Diego was a very sexual being—as was she. Sex was something that had always been brilliant between them.

And he'd turned it down.

Turned *her* down.

Mortifying. Horrifying. It was… It was…

Grace groaned and dropped her head to the desk, crossing her arms over the back of it.

'What's wrong?' Gabbi asked as she swiftly walked up to her, holding an armful of notes and plonking them down on the desk.

Grace sat up. 'What makes you think something is wrong?'

'Women only make noises like that when their spouse or their boss is making their life hell. So which is it?'

Grace smiled. 'Diego.'

'Ah… Want to talk about it?'

She wasn't sure. *Did* she want to discuss her personal life with Gabbi? She almost de-

cided against it, but who else could she talk
to? Gabbi was about her age, and married,
so she might understand.

'You know Diego and I have had a few
issues?'

'He's been sleeping in staff accommodation for a while, so...yeah.'

'Well, we've grown close again over
Zara's case...as you know we've been working together.'

'Uh-huh.' Gabbi swept her hair up into
a knot, sticking it in position with her pen.

'After last night's shift he took me out for
breakfast. It was lovely. We talked, we chatted, we went for a walk over to the basilica.
We lit candles for our babies.' She smiled
sadly. 'And then he walked me home.'

'I feel that it's about to get complicated at
this point.'

Grace grimaced. 'We kissed, and it was
like...' she looked around to make sure no
one else could hear '...a damned good kiss.
Hot. Sexy. The kind of kiss that leads to
more, if you know what I mean?'

'I'm a midwife. I understand how kisses
lead to more. So what happened?'

'He said no, and he walked away. Said
he had to get back to the hospital. I felt...'

She shrugged, recalling exactly how she felt that morning. 'I felt abandoned again. Like I wasn't good enough and that maybe I'd misread the signals, or something. But surely a man doesn't kiss you like that and then just walk away?'

Gabbi sighed, clearly thinking.

'I mean…have I got it all wrong? I thought we were going to be okay. I thought we could save what we'd lost and we were rebuilding our relationship… But he couldn't get away from me fast enough, Gabs.' She could feel the tears. The lump in her throat. The old hurt. The old pain resurfacing, announcing itself with a roar. 'Are we truly over?'

Gabbi reached out a comforting hand. 'Only you and Diego know that. But is it possible that he got scared?'

'Of what? Me?'

'Of what might have happened if he had followed you into the apartment.'

Grace shook her head. 'He's not scared of sex or intimacy, Gabs.'

'Perhaps you need to speak to him?'

'I don't know what to say.'

'I'm sure you'll think of something. Now, don't you have to take Zara up to see her baby?'

'Yes. But what if I get up there and speak to him and he wants to call off the whole thing? End the marriage. Walk away.'

'I'm sorry, honey, I don't know. You two have been through some terrible times. That does damage to a relationship. Did you ever have counselling?'

Grace shook her head. 'No. Not really.'

'You need to talk to him. Look, the floor's not busy right now. Why don't you take Zara up for a visit to the NICU before she goes to sleep, and see if you can speak with him whilst Zara is with her baby?'

Grace nodded. 'Yeah. Thanks, Gabs.'

She got up and headed down to Zara's room, knocking gently before going in.

'How are you feeling?' she asked her.

'Sore.'

'That's to be expected. Have you been getting up? Moving around?'

'A little.'

'Think you could manage a walk up to the NICU?'

Zara nodded, albeit reluctantly. 'Sure.'

'I'll pass you your dressing gown.'

She waited for Zara to be presentable, and then slowly escorted her down the long corridor towards the lift that would take them up a floor to the NICU.

The closer they got, the more the butterflies in Grace's stomach built. She kept picturing herself in those moments after Diego's scorching kiss, smiling up at him, asking him to come inside, and then seeing the look on his face and the way he'd backed away from her—as if he'd just discovered she had the plague, or something!

But she couldn't hide for ever. Problems didn't get solved by hiding from them or avoiding them. That just made them worse.

Their marriage was proof of that.

He saw Grace and Zara come out of the lift and, knowing that they would be heading to see Zara's baby, he decided to stay in his office.

He wasn't hiding. He was simply undecided. Undecided what to say. How to behave. Grace had invited him in, and although every fibre of his being had wanted to accept and go in with her, revisit her body, he had walked away instead.

She must have felt so rejected! And he had no idea if she was angry now or just disappointed, resigned to ending their marriage?

He didn't want that. At all. But he'd known he needed to leave that morning, no matter how much he still loved her and wanted her. He had simply known that it was not the right thing for them to do.

He knew she would be confused by his walking away, but he hoped she'd see the sense in it. Though that kiss they'd shared was etched onto his brain, into his very being, because of how wonderful it had been, he'd known deep inside that to protect this woman he would have to go.

She probably wouldn't understand that, and he couldn't tell her his reasoning right now—neither did he want to bring up the traumatic memories of her miscarriages. This wasn't the time and place. There was no way he wanted to see that hurt in her eyes again. To know that he'd caused it.

No. What he needed to do was wait for the right moment. Keep his distance. Stay away from—

'Hey, there.'

He looked up from his desk and frowned. Grace was standing in the doorway to his office, twiddling her fingers as if she didn't know what to do with her hands.

He felt heat inflame his face as he recalled

his rejection of her. But if they were going to stay friends through this he knew he had to respect her, keep his distance until he could make his message clear—they could not revive their relationship sexually, no matter how much they wanted it. That part was over. Otherwise they'd allow themselves to get carried away. Would believe in the mirage until all the pain got raked up again.

'Hi.' He got up to put a patient file away in the filing cabinet, then went back behind his desk and sat down. 'Can I help you with something?' He tried to keep his tone neutral.

'Zara's with her baby boy. I brought her up to see him before she tries to get some rest.'

He nodded and tapped at his keyboard, bringing up his list of surgeries for the next week and pretending to scan them.

'I just wanted to see how you were doing after...well, you know...'

After the kiss. That was what she meant. Well, he was nearly exploding right now! Did she have any idea how difficult it was to have her this close again, after that kiss this morning? His body was responding to her the way it always did, and the willpower it was taking to control himself and not just march over there and take her in his arms was terrifying.

'I'm fine. Look, I don't mean to be rude, but I'm quite busy and I don't really have time to chat with you. Maybe later?'

He made eye contact with her, keeping his face neutral, so that she knew he wasn't trying to be mean, just that he was busy. *Very* busy. And that he didn't need his very hot English rose of a wife lingering in his doorway, biting her bottom lip and curling her hair behind her ear. It was driving him crazy!

'Of course. Sorry. I'll…er…let you be. I'll be in with Zara if you need me for anything.'

'Fine.' He forced a smile that didn't reach his eyes, his signal to her that she could go.

This was killing him! Being so distant. They'd made up so much ground between them since her return from Cornwall and now he was destroying it all over again! Hurting her again!

Why didn't I just ask to see her later? Arrange a date? No. Not a date. A coffee.

'Right. Okay. Bye, then.'

She was gone before he could clarify.

He watched her retreat and sagged in his chair, unaware of how much tension he'd been holding in his body. What the hell was he doing? Playing with her emotions like this? Moving out, then being friends. Taking her out for a meal. Kissing her, then walking away. Being rude.

It was not how he saw himself. Diego had always prided himself on being a decent guy, always trying to do the right thing for other people. Thinking of others' feelings before his own.

But perhaps he was viewing this all wrong? Just because she'd suggested sex, it didn't necessarily mean she wanted anything else. She hadn't asked anything of him. Perhaps he needed to push his own wants to one side and just maintain his distance from his wife as much as he could.

Either way, once Zara's baby was fixed properly and discharged from the hospital they could both just get on with their lives.

Separately.

Grace walked away from Diego's office feeling her heart crumble into little pieces. He could not have made it clearer. The kiss had been a mistake and so had she, and he had no intention of making things right between them.

She had to accept that it was over.

Grace wiped at her eyes and took a few deep breaths before she entered the room where Zara sat beside her baby.

'Hey, how's he doing?'

'He looks awful. I can see his intestines. It's just so *wrong*!'

'He won't be like that for ever. Once the swelling goes down Diego will be able to put them back.'

And once Zara's baby had his medical condition corrected she and Diego would have no reason to work so closely on a case together.

'This is my fault. I knew I was pregnant and I never took any of those vitamin things, or had myself checked out! I caused this!'

'No. No, you didn't. This condition happens to babies with mothers who follow all the rules! You can take your vitamins, you can rest and not overdo it, you can eat the right foods, avoid alcohol and soft cheese and whatever else they tell you to avoid, and it can still go wrong.' She thought of all the rules *she'd* followed. Especially the second time. And the third time she'd got pregnant she'd been almost afraid to move. 'You can't blame yourself.'

Zara looked at her, and then down at her baby. 'I haven't held him yet.'

'Do you want to? I'm sure if I asked a nurse we'd be able to find a way.'

She shook her head. 'No. I don't want to hurt him any more than I already have.'

Grace laid a comforting hand on Zara's. 'Just give him your love, Zara. That's all he needs.'

She'd thought giving all her love to Diego would be enough. But love hadn't fixed the fact that she'd stopped him from having the large family of his dreams. Love hadn't fixed the fact that their marriage was most definitely doomed.

That kiss had been a lapse in judgement, and Diego was trying to make that clear without saying so outright.

I need to face facts.

'Have you heard?' Gabbi asked as Grace came onto her shift the next night.

'Heard what?'

'Zara's baby… Diego has said he's ready to go back in for the final surgery to reduce his exomphalos.'

Grace pressed her backpack into her locker,

closing it. 'That's fabulous news. When did you hear that?'

'Day shift told me. I think he's waiting for you, so you can both go in and tell Zara the news together.'

Grace nodded. It was good of him to wait. He could have told Zara alone. 'Right. Okay. Is he on this floor?'

'I think he's in with Renata.'

'I guess I ought to go and find him, then.'

Letting out an anxious sigh, she straightened her uniform and headed down the corridor towards Renata's office. As she passed, the door to Zara's room was open, and for the first time she was dressed in normal clothes instead of a hospital gown.

Grace said hello and gave her a wave. 'We'll be in to talk to you in a moment. Looks like Diego can finish your son's surgery. Don't go anywhere.'

And then she was past Zara's room and at Renata's office. The door was open and Grace's boss was inside, having a chat with Diego.

'Grace! We were just discussing you.'

'All good things, I hope.' She glanced at Diego, but he didn't meet her gaze, and she felt the hurt hit her right in the solar plexus.

'I was just informing Renata that I'm going to take Zara's baby up to Theatre.'

She nodded. 'I heard.'

'You've been involved in the case from the beginning. It would be remiss of me not to invite you to see the surgery through.' His voice was neutral and he barely looked at her, clearly uncomfortable with being in the same room as her.

It made her feel a little angry. 'Thank you. I'd like that.'

And maybe they could talk? In Theatre he couldn't back away from her, could he? But would he appreciate her discussing their failing relationship in front of the scrub nurses, the neonatal team that he had to work with, and the anaesthetist?

Probably not.

It would be embarrassing to start off with, and completely unkind. But she wanted to tell him so much about how rejected he was making her feel, and she just couldn't see when they'd get a chance to talk again.

As they walked down the corridor side by side she felt…small. As if somehow she'd lost who she truly was, as if part of her was missing, and she knew that missing part was wrapped up in Diego still. How to tell him that he'd dashed her dreams of reuniting? That his cool tone had broken her heart? That if they couldn't do this and be friends then she most definitely would be leaving— because she couldn't stand to stay here and be spoken to as if she had never been anything more than a colleague?

But then they were at Zara's room and it was empty, the covers half thrown off the bed, the room in disarray.

Grace frowned. 'She was here just a second ago.' She looked at the door to the ensuite bathroom, which was closed. 'Maybe she's in the bathroom?' she knocked on the door. 'Zara? It's Grace and Diego.'

But there was no answer.

Diego looked down at the door to the Vacant/Engaged sign. 'It's not locked.'

Had she collapsed inside the bathroom?

Grace knocked again. 'We're coming in!' she said, and yanked open the door—only to find that the bathroom was empty, too. Puzzled, she turned to look at Diego. 'Where is she?'

He shook his head. 'I don't know.'

'I saw her just seconds ago. I told her we were coming in to talk to her about her baby's surgery.'

'Could she have gone up to the NICU?'

That seemed the most likely answer. She must have felt she needed to see him before he went into Theatre and hadn't wanted to wait for Diego and Grace. Felt that every second she could spend with him would be precious, just in case.

They didn't bother waiting for a lift. They both raced up the stairs, Diego's longer strides taking the stairs two at a time, before they burst out onto the NICU floor. Diego slid his card through the security reader and they headed for the room where Zara's baby lay.

She wasn't there either.

'Have you seen Zara Rodriguez?' he asked one of his nurses, who shook her head before going to look at the visitors' log.

'The last time she came up to see him was at lunchtime today. She didn't stay long. Only five minutes.'

'How did she seem?' asked Grace, feeling a terrible sense of doom approaching.

'Weird. A nurse has written a request for a follow-up check for postnatal depression.'

Grace looked at Diego. 'She could still be in the hospital. She might be just…'

'Might be what?'

'I don't know. But we need to look for her inside before we assume anything bad.'

'I'll alert Security.'

She watched him stride over to the desk and pick up the phone, giving a description of Zara and asking for anyone who spotted her to notify Diego immediately. When he got off the phone, he came back to her.

'So where do you think she might have gone?'

'Let's go back to her room one last time, then let's check the café—or even outside in the gardens.'

'Okay. How did she seem when you told her we were coming to talk about her son's surgery?'

'I don't know. It was said in passing as I came to find you. She looked…' Grace thought back to that tiny glimpse of Zara. Wearing street clothes. Trainers on. When Grace had said they were going to talk about the surgery she'd looked… 'Scared. She looked terrified.'

'I think she's done a runner.'

'She wouldn't leave her baby, Diego!'

'Wouldn't she?'

She opened her mouth to speak, to answer, to reprimand him for his outrageous suggestion, but a tiny voice inside told her that he could be right. Some mothers did abandon their children. They did it because they couldn't cope. Or they did it because they thought the child would have a better chance in life with someone else. Or they did it because that had been the plan all along. They couldn't afford to keep a child, so they gave birth and then they left.

But Zara hadn't left the second her baby had been born. She had stayed. She had visited him. Grace was convinced she cared about her son. Loved him the way that Grace had loved and wanted her own babies. Only now it was crunch time and she'd got scared.

They began searching the maternity wing but found nothing. They searched the NICU again, but there was no sign of her. Then Diego's mobile phone rang.

'Hello?'

Grace watched him listen, then turn to her as he put his phone back in his pocket.

'She was spotted in the security feed leaving the hospital and heading towards St Aelina's Park.'

Grace stared back at him. 'The folly... Isabella found her at the folly when she was first brought in.'

'Let's go.'

They went down the floors in a lift and then ran out into the cool evening air. Lights were coming on across the city, and though it was still busy it was nothing like it was in the daytime.

'Where is the folly?' Diego asked.

'I don't know. I've never really explored the park.'

There were signposts directing them to certain paths, but it seemed to her that they were going in circles for ages—until she finally spotted a sign saying Secret Folly in both Spanish and Catalan.

'This way.'

It had been a long time since Grace had done any running, and by the time they arrived at the folly she was completely out of breath. But as they rounded the south-east path that brought them to the stone building they both saw a dejected-looking Zara, sitting on its steps, looking out over the lake. They slowed to a walk.

'Zara?' Grace called.

Zara turned to look at them and they could see the tears in her eyes. When she saw them she looked embarrassed and turned away, wiping the tear stains from her face. 'You must think that I am a terrible mother.'

'No. Of course not. You're just scared.'

'It's just that…he's so little, and he's already been through so much, and I don't want to be responsible for putting him through more surgery so soon. What if he dies? What if I lose him? He's all I've got.'

They sat either side of her, Grace taking her hand in hers. 'It's natural to be scared. But you can't leave him as he is. He needs that surgery, and he needs his mother to be there waiting for him when he comes out the other side.'

'Grace is right,' Diego said, his tone soft. 'He needs his mother to be strong for him. That's all any child needs from a parent. For them to believe in them, to love them and to protect them. You can do all of those things.'

Zara shook her head. 'I've already run from him. I tried not to visit him too often because it hurt to look at him like that, and now… Now I've run away from him. I abandoned him. I could never be a good mother.'

'My guess is you've never been shown what a good mother can be,' said Diego. 'Maybe that's why you chose to live on the streets. Who knows? But what I do know is that you are a mother who wants the best for her son. You want him to live, don't you?'

'Of course I do!'

'You didn't not visit him because you didn't care,' Diego went on. 'In fact you cared so much you couldn't bear to see him suffering. That hurt you. Left scars in your heart that will never go. I know what it is to feel that way, Zara. I understand. Sometimes you love someone so strongly, with an all-or-nothing love, that when you see them suffering it tears out your heart, so you think the only answer is to run. To get away. To hide from it. But you're wrong. It's the worst thing you can do. And you're not alone. You don't have to do this alone. Grace and I will help you find somewhere to live. We can set you up with support groups and maybe even some financial aid, so that you can give your son the kind of life you want him to have. A normal one. Just like anyone else's.'

Grace felt her eyes well up at Diego's words. What had he said? That he knew what it was like to see someone suffering? That it left scars in your heart? That when you saw someone you loved suffering you thought the only thing to do was to run from it?

He was talking about *them*.

'You don't know this yet, Zara,' he said, 'but you are brave and strong. And although a love like this makes you want to run from it, because of its overwhelming nature, you will embrace it—because it is yours and it belongs to you and no one else. That little boy back in the hospital has no one but you. He needs you and you need him.'

Grace wiped away a tear at his words. The fact that he could speak so eloquently and show that he was capable of understanding such intense emotions when she'd once thought him so barren of them… Well, that left scars on *her* heart. For thinking badly of him. For thinking that he was unfeeling and shallow.

Diego felt things. He might never express those feelings outright, but they were there and that gave her hope.

'That feeling you're experiencing right now is something so unique, so rare, and it's also the one reason that makes you stay. It's *love*, Zara. And you *love* your baby.'

Zara threw her arms around Diego, surprising him. Grace watched them both.

Proud of Diego. Proud of Zara. She'd learned something about both of them today.

She wanted to tell Diego she understood now. Understood why he'd run from her. Why he'd turned his back. But this wasn't the right time or place, so she tried to break the tension another way. 'Anyone know the short route back to the hospital?' she asked with a smile.

Zara nodded, letting go of Diego with a thank-you. 'I do.'

'I'll be with you in a minute,' Grace said to Diego as he went to prep for surgery.

She watched him walk away, feeling all different kinds of emotions, seeing the world with new eyes. Diego hadn't left her because he didn't care. He'd left her because he couldn't bear to see her in so much pain.

Why hadn't he just told her that? Why put her through the torment of making her feel that she wasn't good enough? That she was failing in her duties as a wife to provide him with children?

Why couldn't they have just talked about it?

She got Zara settled in her room again. 'I'll be in Theatre with Diego. When we can, we'll send a nurse out with updates, to keep you informed on how it's going. Okay?'

Zara nodded.

'We're going to take good care of him.'

'I know.'

'Just don't run. Stay. Can you do that?'

'Yes.'

'Okay.'

Grace was about to go when Zara spoke again.

'Are you and Diego okay?'

'I'm sorry?' Grace pretended she hadn't heard. She didn't normally discuss her private life with patients.

'You're married, right? Only, there's a tension between you two. I've noticed it. I only mention it because…well, Diego is going in there to operate on my son, and I need to know that he's in the right frame of mind to do so. I appreciate all that you've both done for me. How you've put yourselves out for me. But that's my baby boy in there, and I need to know he's in the right hands.'

Grace let out a sigh. 'We've had a few issues, I'll admit. But we're okay. And when Diego is in that theatre our personal lives don't follow him in. He'll focus on the patient on the table—they always come first. I don't want you to worry.'

'I will, though. Until I know he's all right.'

'I know.'

'And it will all be over? After this surgery no more? I'll be able to hold him and he can be a normal baby?'

Grace smiled. 'He can be a normal baby and you can be a normal mum.'

She headed off towards the theatre, feeling proud of how far Zara had come—from the surly teenager she'd first met in the ER to the caring mother she saw now, who'd been at her wits' end with worry.

Zara's case had shone a light on her relationship with Diego in ways she could never have expected. She felt she understood her husband a little more now. But although she wanted to talk to him about it she'd promised Zara she would not bring anything personal into Theatre. She would wait until afterwards and ask to speak to him then. Clear the air.

In the scrub room, she reached for a scrub pack, cleaning her nails with the pick and brush, then washing her hands with water and the special antimicrobial soap, up to her elbows. Through the viewing window she saw Diego, already in Theatre, being helped into his gown and gloves, and their tiny patient, already anaesthetised, lying on the table.

Zara's fears about losing her child were understandable. Grace knew that more than most. And so did Diego...

Heading into Theatre, mask already in place, Grace smiled at Diego. 'Ready?'

He nodded. 'And raring to go.'

'Okay. Let's do this. Let's give Zara a healthy baby.'

She stood back, opposite him, beneath the theatre lights.

'Scalpel.'

The scrub nurse placed the blade into his hand.

As the surgery began, Grace watched her husband with new eyes. Once again falling in love with the man behind the mask, who saved babies' lives every single day. That he had the skills and the talent to do so was remarkable, and it was something about him that she adored. He moved adeptly, cleanly, each practised move sure and steady, as if he'd done this a million times.

She watched as he reduced the exomphalos and began to put the intestines inside the baby boy's abdomen.

I'm going to talk to him when this is over.

I'm going to tell him that I understand him now.

I'm going to tell him that there's still a chance for us if he wants me.

She wasn't fearful about putting herself out there and having him reject her. She'd done that before and she'd survived. This time it would be different.

You had to be brave when it came to love.

You had to be willing to step out of your comfort zone and put your heart on the line.

Because loving someone meant you had to be vulnerable. You had to be open.

And she loved this man and wasn't willing to let him go any more.

And when this surgery was over she would reveal her heart to him, knowing that he would reach for it and take her back.

Of course he would.

He wouldn't have said those words before if he didn't want to.

He'd shown her, through Zara, that he'd suffered too. That he'd run away from her because he'd been protecting *himself.*

I did the same thing when I ran away to Cornwall.

They'd both made mistakes.

The important thing was to admit them...

CHAPTER NINE

THE SURGERY WAS going smoothly, but Diego was struggling internally. Outwardly, he was like a swan. Calm, graceful. But underneath his heart was pounding and his mind was racing.

All those things he'd said in the park to Zara, to get her to come back to the hospital… he'd said them in front of Grace. Exposing parts of himself he'd never meant to show her because they would hurt her, too. Remind her of their past. Their terrible, painful, grief-wrecked past. Would reveal to her that when he saw someone suffering he wanted to run…

Embarrassing. He'd shown himself to be weak—she must think him a terrible fool. She had to be wondering what she'd ever seen in him. How she could have been with someone who didn't have the strength to stay when life got tough.

It was pitiful.

But the words had simply poured forth. He'd seen Zara suffering and had understood her fear of the unknown, her fear of the surgery, her fear of not being good enough.

He knew that last one too well.

All he'd wanted to do was let her know that she wasn't alone. That she wasn't the only person ever to feel that way and that she was strong—that she did have it inside her to carry on, because he'd seen it in her. She was someone who had the ability to stay alive on the streets and not use alcohol or drugs to numb the pain of being unwanted. That took huge reserves and he knew she had more inside. He'd just wanted to remind her of that…that was all.

But then he'd exposed parts of himself he'd always thought he would keep hidden. He'd run from Grace not just because he hadn't been able to bear to see her suffer, but because seeing her suffer had made him feel…helpless.

Helpless was not a feeling that Diego often associated with himself. He had lost his parents early. Isabella had helped protect them all, but he'd been the eldest boy and he'd often felt he needed to be the man of the house. He'd taken on responsibility at an early age. He was used to being strong, to being the one who coped, who remained stoic and in control, because that was what everyone needed to see. Someone who didn't panic. Someone who didn't fall apart at the slightest hiccup.

He'd become a neonatal surgeon because it needed the utmost confidence. Not everyone could find the nerve to operate on a newborn baby, using tiny instruments on tiny organs and tiny arteries and nerves. He'd wanted to show he could compete with the best because he'd always felt like the best.

Until his wife had lost a baby. And then another. And then another.

He'd spent a lifetime proving he could save babies, but he'd never been able to save his own. That changed a man like him. Saving babies was his reason for being. Every baby saved was a life saved. A family saved.

Losing his three children had lost him his wife and his family.

Watching his wife fall apart, watching his marriage fall apart, had not been something he could handle. Observing what it did to him when he saw his wife bent double, sobbing with pain and grief, had not been something he could deal with at all—because what was he supposed to do?

Hugs and cuddles had been useless. They hadn't made things right. They hadn't brought their babies back. And his words had seemed empty.

So he'd stopped using them.

It had been easier to return to work and prove that he *wasn't* helpless—because at work he could be a god. He could save lives and restore limbs and remove tumours and give people the healthy babies that they deserved. He could help everyone else.

Except Grace and himself.

When this surgery was done…when they got Zara settled into a place where she could live securely…then his time with Grace would be over. He would be able to get that distance again. Maybe even apply for a transfer to somewhere else? He'd always fancied seeing the world. Seeing how they did things in different countries. Cairo would be good. Maybe Saigon? Or Cambodia. Somewhere far, far away from Barcelona.

It would give Grace the space she needed too. Neither of them could breathe with the other so close. Living and working in each other's pockets only served to confuse them even more, and caused them to make mistakes—like on that morning when he'd kissed her outside their old apartment.

The thought of that kiss made him briefly look up at his wife, standing opposite him across the operating table. That kiss had been…something else. She was so beautiful. So perfect. But he'd failed her and she didn't deserve that. He loved her enough to let her go and find happiness with someone who could give her the babies she wanted. He'd been wrong to try to hold onto her.

I'll do that for her. Because I've got to be the strong one.

With the exomphalos reduced and all the internal organs inside the boy's abdomen, where they should have been all along, Diego began to sew up the small abdominal hole. He let Grace snip the final suture.

'Done.' He looked at her from behind his mask and nodded. It was done. He couldn't allow himself to think *what if?* any more.

'Let's keep him in the NICU for a few more days' monitoring, but I don't see any reason why his mum can't give him that first cuddle.' He went to step away from the table, pulling at his gloves and gown.

'Diego? Do you have a moment?'

He closed his eyes in pain at hearing Grace's voice. She wanted something. Clearly she did. But he had nothing left to give her now. He couldn't. He had to forbid himself from thinking he could give her anything again.

'No, I'm sorry.' He began to walk away.

'Diego!'

He turned. 'Grace. No. No more. We've done enough.'

And he walked away, hoping that she would finally get the message, even though his heart was breaking and tears burned the backs of his eyes.

Grace stood there, cheeks flaming in shame, surprise, and more than anything else anger.

That was it? He was *done?* He thought that he had the power to decide when they were over all by himself?

How could they be over? He'd said all those things...

She'd thought it was his way of telling her he was sorry and that they would be moving on. A new beginning for both of them. *Together.*

She watched him go, walking away from her without looking back. The set of his shoulders certainly made him look as if he was fed up with all the nonsense and that he was done. Just *done*.

How many times would he break her heart?

How many times would she *allow* him to break her heart?

This wasn't good enough. She deserved more. She deserved her moment in the sun and to say exactly what she wanted to say to him.

But first Zara. Grace needed to go to her and tell her how the surgery had gone, then take her up to see her baby. Let them have that first cuddle. That was more important than any grudge she had with Diego. He could wait. He wasn't going anywhere.

She removed her own gloves and gown, scrubbed down, and then went in search of Zara. Grace found her in her room, sitting in a high-backed chair, looking anxious.

When she saw Grace she got to her feet. 'Is it done? How is he?'

Grace smiled. 'It's all done and he's absolutely fine. Do you want to go and see him?'

Zara let out a pent-up breath and then rushed into Grace's arms, crying and sobbing, thanking her for getting her through it. For getting her son through it.

'It wasn't me. It was Diego.'

'Where is he? I want to thank him.'

What could she say? She didn't know. 'I think he got called to another case,' she lied. 'But it all went perfectly.'

She walked Zara up to the NICU, her stomach churning at the thought of seeing her husband again, but he was nowhere to be seen.

When Zara was sitting with her son in her arms for the first time, Grace grabbed hold of a passing nurse. 'Where's Dr Rivas?'

'I think he's left already. Said he needed some time away.'

Grace smiled and thanked her, the smile dropping from her face the second the nurse turned from her.

He needed 'time away'?

She knew where he would be. The place he always went when he wanted time to think away from the hospital. The beach. She checked her watch. Soon the sun would rise. He'd gone for that. He'd always said he found watching the sun rise soothing.

'How does it feel?' she asked Zara, looking at her holding her son for the first time ever.

'Amazing! He's so perfect! So small!'

'When you hold your baby in your arms for the first time it changes you, doesn't it?'

As always, Grace felt a little spike of envy. The only baby of hers that she'd held in her arms was Luca. Stillborn. So, so tiny. So, so still. She had no idea what it would be like to hold a baby that was not only hers, but alive and breathing. A baby that would look up at her face and yawn, or sneeze, or give a little crooked windy smile.

Her whole body ached at the thought.

Her story couldn't be over. *Their* story couldn't be over. Not yet. Neither of them had *tried.* They'd both just given up when the going got tough and that wasn't them.

At that moment Renata tapped on the window of the unit to get Grace's attention.

Sucking in a deep breath, she excused herself for a minute and popped outside to see her superior. 'What's up?'

'I've just had a call from a women's shelter that has a space for Zara and her baby.

Just a one-bedroom place in El Poblenou, but it's hers if she wants it.'

'Really? That's amazing. I'm sure she'll say yes. Would you accept it for her?'

'Of course.' Renata looked in at Zara. 'It all went well, then?'

Grace smiled and nodded. 'Yes.'

'And for you?'

Now she frowned. 'How do you mean?'

'You and Diego? I know you've been having problems, and I didn't want to pry, but... I'm short-staffed, and I really don't want to lose my best midwife if you decide to return home.'

Grace was stunned. She hadn't realised that everyone knew. But should it be a surprise? Gossip mills in hospitals picked up on any kind of rumour, and she and Diego could easily have been overheard in this place.

'I haven't decided anything yet.'

'But you'll let me know? As soon as you can? I'd hate to lose you, Grace.'

Grace gave her a sudden hug. A thank-you, for showing that she cared. That she didn't see Grace as just another employee, but as a valued member of the team whom she didn't want to lose.

'Of course I will.'

Renata wiped away a small tear and squared her shoulders before walking away.

Grace watched her go, then went back into the unit and told Zara about the housing opportunity.

'Wow! I can't thank you enough. You and Diego have done so much for us.'

'It's no problem.'

'No, don't downplay it. I was a street kid. Mouthy, surly. I didn't trust anybody. But you showed me that people care. You both went out of your way to look after me and my son. You saved the only family I have. You gave me a future. I just hope that you and Diego have one too.'

For the second time in moments Grace was stunned. 'Thanks.'

'I don't know what your problems are with each other, but to me you guys are amazing. And I'm sure whatever your problems are you can solve them if you just talk to one another and look for the good. It's so easy to focus on the bad all the time that we can forget the good times.'

Grace stared at Zara, wondering how such a young street kid had got so wise. But she was right. She'd spent so long focusing on all the bad things in her and Diego's relationship she'd forgotten the good times—and there'd been plenty of those.

Lazy mornings in bed, when neither of them had had to work. Cooking together in the kitchen, testing long strings of pasta by feeding them to one another, laughing. Snatching moments together at work in between cases, when just seeing him had given her the extra burst of energy she'd needed to get through a shift. Shopping together... browsing old markets and bookstores. Going out on a boat that time for their first wedding anniversary, intending to sunbathe and have a champagne picnic only to discover that Diego got seasick. Watching movies. Sharing ice cream in that small café in Sarrià.

Marrying him—even if it had been a small ceremony with just a couple of witnesses. Standing there next to him, holding a small bunch of flowers that they'd bought from a florist's beforehand, looking into his dark brown eyes and promising him for ever.

For ever.

She'd meant it when she'd made her vows, as brief as they'd been. She'd stood there, holding those flowers, promising herself to him for the rest of her life and she'd meant it. She couldn't let him walk away like this.

She needed to remind him of the promises they had made.

And, okay, maybe they'd made those promises to each other when they'd thought life would be easy for them, and that there wouldn't be any problems with having babies, but surely she still had value to him? She couldn't have just been a womb to him—a means to get the family he wanted. He must have fallen in love with her, and not just her ability to have a family...or not.

She turned back to Zara. 'If you're all settled here, I've got some things I need to do. You'll be okay?'

Zara nodded. 'I'm going to be fine now. We both are.'

'I'll come and check on you later, okay?'

Zara nodded, but her attention was already back on her son, just as it should be.

Grace quietly slipped from the room.

His marriage was well and truly over. He'd never thought he'd be the one to sound the death knell, but someone had needed to be strong enough to do so. He'd never expected this ache inside. This hollowness. This emptiness that he felt in his chest—as if someone had ripped out his heart and all that was left was the empty cage where it had once been kept.

He tried to tell himself that he had tried to save their marriage, but knew he wasn't fully telling himself the truth. Diego tore off his tie and flung it into the nearest bin, opened up his shirt and headed onto the sand. He needed to feel it, so he kicked off his shoes, pulled off his socks, rolled up his trousers and walked across the cool sand towards the water.

The sun had not yet risen, but it would soon, and when it did it would rise on a new day. A new beginning. A day that promised many seconds, minutes and hours for him to fill in his new life as a single man.

It was not a joyous thought. He'd loved being married. Adored being dedicated to one woman. To Grace. She'd been every-thing he'd ever wanted in a woman…and now he'd walked away from her for the final time.

It felt…wrong. It felt painful. But it was a sensation he was used to because that was what he did, time and time again, when things got tough. He walked away. He shut down and threw himself into work, where his life *could* be successful. He used work as a balm. A soothing agent to make him feel better.

I should have turned to Grace to make myself feel better. Only I couldn't because she was hurting too.

He kept telling himself that he'd been trying to protect her, but in all honesty he knew he'd actually been trying to protect himself, too. Why not claim he was being the strong one if it made him feel even a tiny bit better? Why not lie to himself?

Because lying to myself hasn't exactly worked out, has it?

Lying to himself had caused him to end up on this beach alone.

He stared out across the dark water, feeling it lap at his ankles, the coldness enveloping his lower legs, his toes sinking into the wet sand beneath.

Lying to myself caused me to lie to her.

She ran through the streets, knowing he would be at the beach, waiting for the sun to rise. It was his thing when he was troubled. He said it always helped clear his head of muddled thinking when he was stressed about work or a project or a patient. He'd begun going after each baby was lost. She

had to assume he was there now, because…
Well, because there were still some things
that needed to be said.

Grace did not want to let her marriage go
unless she'd told him exactly how she felt.
If he still decided it was over after all that
then she would have to accept it—because
you couldn't *make* someone love you. She
would walk away if she had to, but right now
she felt that there was still a chance.

She'd seen a sliver of the real Diego when
he'd talked Zara into coming back to the
hospital, and then there'd been that kiss,
too, showing that somewhere inside he still
had feelings for her. So, this wasn't over. It
couldn't be over until Diego was in full pos-
session of the facts.

The street lamps were still on and there
were hardly any people out and about at
this early hour. She heard her feet slapping
against the pavement as she ran towards the
promenade, her gaze scanning the dark horizon, looking for him in the darkness.

She stopped, panting heavily, not knowing why it felt so urgent that she had to tell
him how she felt right now. Maybe because
so much time had been lost between them
already and she didn't want to miss any more

unless she absolutely had to. She had to try everything. And then, if it didn't work out, she would at least know that she had given her all.

There. Out by the water's edge. A solitary figure stood. It looked like him. The stance. She'd know him anywhere.

Letting out one long breath, she began to walk across the sand, at one point pulling off her shoes and walking barefoot, carrying her shoes in her hand.

She could hear the gentle lapping of the water. Her stomach twisted into knots as she approached, trying to think of what she should say first. What was important? What did he actually need to hear? It seemed impossible to settle on one actual thing and her pace slowed as she neared him, suddenly uncertain and unsure. If this went wrong... if he rejected her one more time...could she bear it?

Grace stood alongside her husband, about a metre apart from him, staring out to the dark sea. To the horizon, already beginning to turn a lighter blue, with hints of orange and red as the sun started to rise.

'I thought I'd find you here.'

She sensed him turn to look at her and she

knew that it was important, in that moment, that she didn't meet his gaze. She continued to look out at the array of colours beginning to slowly materialise in the sky.

He let out a sigh and she panicked. Was he about to tell her that she should never have followed him here?

'How's Zara?'

Relief. 'She's very happy. She was holding her baby when I left. And Renata came. Told me she'd found a home Zara can have when she gets discharged.'

'That's good. A home is important.'

She nodded, risking a glance at him now. His tie was gone, his shirt unbuttoned…his trousers were rolled up and he was barefoot. She saw no sign of his shoes and briefly wondered what he had done with them.

'You always wanted a beach wedding.' He turned to face her. Waited for her to meet his gaze. 'I wish I'd given that to you. I wish…' He sighed, looked down. 'I wish I'd done a lot of things differently.'

Grace felt her breath catch. 'Me too.'

'I wish I'd never thrown myself into work. I wish I'd never stopped talking to you. I wish that things had been different.'

There was a massive lump in her throat suddenly, making it difficult to talk. 'Me too.'

'I used work as an escape, didn't I? But you need to know, Grace, that I didn't use it to escape *you*. I used it to escape having to confront the emotions that I was feeling staying at home. Your pain, your grief, just made me feel *powerless*! And that wasn't something that sat easy with me.'

She listened intently, feeling all the old emotions swimming to the surface.

'I wanted to hold you. I wanted to tell you that everything would be all right. But how could I? When evidence wasn't there to show us that we could have the family that we both dreamed of? You didn't seem to want me after life kept telling us no. My words, my actions, felt empty, so I simply stopped—because of how it made me feel. I was so busy fighting off feeling impotent that I forgot you were still suffering. No.' He shook his head. 'I still knew... I just felt I couldn't do anything about it—and that was wrong. I'm sorry. I'm *so* sorry!'

He turned away from her, looked out at the first glimpse of sun as it emerged over the horizon.

'I don't blame you for leaving me. I don't blame you for walking away. Because we weren't happy any more. And I was the one who had made you sad. I was the one who had caused you pain. I couldn't protect you, or our babies. I accept now that I have to let you go, so that you can find the happiness you deserve with someone else.'

'*No!*' The word came out of her with such strength, such force, it surprised her. 'I'm not leaving you, Diego. You didn't cause me this pain. I couldn't carry our babies to term—that was just sheer bad luck. It wasn't your fault. And, yes, you pulled away from me, but I pulled away from you, too. Don't you see? *I* felt guilty. *I* was the one who couldn't carry your babies. *I* was the one who couldn't meet your eye because of the guilt that I felt. *I* was the one who caused you pain. I pulled away from you when you tried to help. I shut down even as I watched our marriage fall apart, I did nothing to save it. I let you down, Diego.'

She took a step towards him. And then another. And another.

He looked at her uncertainly, and so she did what she knew she would have to do to show him that her love for him was still there if he wanted it. She slipped her arms around him and looked up into his eyes.

'Yes, we stopped being happy with each other—because I think neither of us knew what to do to make the other feel better. We've both had time away now, and I think it's helped us to see…well, it's helped *me* to see…that I miss you terribly and just how much I still love you. We're equally to blame for not communicating with each other. I should have told you how I was feeling when I lost our babies. I should have listened to you to find out how you felt. But when you're in the depths of grief you sometimes forget about others. I became so used to hiding my feelings that I forgot how to show them. But spending all these nights together, working on Zara's case… I feel… I feel it's given us a second chance. If we want to take it. *Do* you, Diego? Do you want to take a second chance on me? Because I'm here for you. I want to try. I love you so much.'

Diego smiled down at her, wiping her tears from her eyes. 'I love you, too. Can we do it, do you think? Are we strong enough? What if it happens again?'

Grace smiled. 'We make a vow. Right now. That we'll make time every day to talk to one another. To tell each other how we're feeling even if it's just about work.'

'And what about…the babies?'

'We talk about them, too. We loved all three of them. And they were gone much too soon. But we *should* talk about them. They were real. They were loved. We had hopes and dreams for each of them and no matter how hard it is we'll talk. I promise you.'

'I'm so sorry I hurt you, Grace. I never want to do that ever again.'

She smiled. 'Ditto.'

'I love you, and I'm never going to let you drift away from me ever again.'

'I love you, too.'

And he bent his head to kiss her as the full glory of the sun rose above the horizon, lighting the sky in a fanfare of orange, red and yellow.

A new beginning for a love that had never died.

EPILOGUE

THE LAST FEW weeks had been a whirlwind of preparation and planning, but somehow they had managed to pull it off.

The beach looked perfect. The perfect backdrop to their event. A white pergola had been erected in front of the water, its trellis interwoven with white flowers. Roses, dahlias, peonies, carnations and tulips. Snapdragons hung from the centre arch, along with gypsophila to make it look ethereal.

Wooden boarding had created a walkway down the centre of the rows of chairs that were now filled with guests for the renewal of their vows.

Grace could see Diego standing at the end of the aisle, waiting for her, along with his best man and the minister.

Had she felt this nervous at her actual wedding?

She could see their friends from the hospital were there too. Santiago, Carlos, Javier, Caitlin… Her colleagues Renata, Gabbi, Ana, Mira—even Olivia, back from her mother's in Andalusia. And on the front row, for the first time, Diego's family. The people she'd always hoped to meet. There was Isabella—whom she already knew, of course—but there was also Eduardo and Luis, looking like younger versions of Diego, and his other sisters Paola and Frida.

This was the big family ceremony she'd always dreamed of and her happiness knew no bounds. Even Zara was there, with her baby boy Jacobo.

Grace stood listening for the violinists to begin playing their music, waiting for her walk down the aisle. It was a shame there was no one to escort her, but—

'Want to take my arm?'

Grace turned and gasped. 'Aunt Felicity!' She threw her arms around her and hugged her. 'How come you're here?'

'Diego told me you were renewing your vows and he paid for my flight out here.' Her aunt gave her a big smile and looked her up and down. 'You look the perfect bride. You're beautiful.'

Grace smiled and slipped her arm through hers.

'Are you ready?' asked her aunt.

'I am.'

Aunt Felicity gave a nod to the violinists and they began their music.

At the end of the aisle Diego turned to look at her, and she saw a broad smile cross his face, his eyes lighting up at the sight of her.

Her heart leapt at seeing him. She had never felt so happy, and she knew that this happiness was more important than any she had ever felt before. Because this happiness—she and Diego had earned it. They had walked through fire with each other. And although life had tried to ruin what they had, they'd somehow survived and fought hard to keep what had drawn them together.

Their love.

As she stood there in front of all their friends and family, holding his hands, saying her vows, she knew this was the happiest day of her life. And that no matter what—even if their future didn't include children—she and Diego were lucky to have such intense